7 BILLION LIVES ARE IN DANGER.
13 STRANGERS WITH TERRIFYING NIGHTMARES.
1 ENEMY WILL STOP AT NOTHING TO DESTROY US ALL.

MY NAME IS SAM.
I AM ONE OF THE LAST THIRTEEN.
OUR BATTLE CONTINUES . . .

This one's for my dad—JP.

Scholastic Canada Ltd.
604 King Street West, Toronto, Ontario M5V 1E1, Canada

Scholastic Inc.
557 Broadway, New York, NY 10012, USA

Scholastic Australia Pty Limited
PO Box 579, Gosford, NSW 2250, Australia

Scholastic New Zealand Limited
Private Bag 94407, Botany, Manukau 2163, New Zealand

Scholastic Children's Books
Euston House, 24 Eversholt Street, London NW1 1DB, UK

www.scholastic.ca

Library and Archives Canada Cataloguing in Publication
Phelan, James, 1979-, author
    11 / by James Phelan.
(The last thirteen)
Issued in print and electronic formats.
ISBN 978-1-4431-2484-3 (pbk.).-ISBN 978-1-4431-3310-4 (html)
    I. Title. II. Title: Eleven. III. Series: Phelan, James, 1979- .
Last thirteen.
PZ7.P52El 2014   j823'.92   C2013-905347-6
                                          C2013-905348-4

First published by Scholastic Australia in 2013. This edition published by Scholastic Canada Ltd. in 2014.
Text copyright © 2013 by James Phelan. Illustrations & design copyright © 2013 by Scholastic Australia.
Illustrations by Chad Mitchell. Design by Nicole Stofberg.

Cover photography: Blueprint © istockphoto.com/Adam Korzekwa; Parkour Tic-Tac © istockphoto.com/Willie B. Thomas; Climbing wall © istockphoto.com/microgen; Leonardo da Vinci (Sepia) © istockphoto.com/pictore; Gears © istockphoto.com/-Oxford-; Mechanical blueprint © istockphoto.com/teekid; Circuit board © istockphoto.com/Bjorn Meyer; Map © istockphoto.com/alengo; Grunge drawing © istockphoto.com/aleksandar velasevic; World map © istockphoto.com/Maksim Pasko; Internet © istockphoto.com/Andrey Prokhorov; Inside clock © istockphoto.com/LdF; Space galaxy © istockphoto.com/Sergii Tsololo; Sunset © istockphoto.com/Joakim Leroy; Blue flare © istockphoto.com/YouraPechkin; Global communication © istockphoto.com/chadive samanthakamani; Earth satellites © istockphoto.com/Alexey Popov; Girl portrait © istockphoto.com/peter zelei; Student & board © istockphoto.com/zhang bo; Young man serious © istockphoto.com/Jacob Wackerhausen; Portrait man © istockphoto.com/Alina Solovyova-Vincent; Sad expression © istockphoto.com/Shelly Perry; Content man © istockphoto.com/drbimages; Pensive man © istockphoto.com/Chuck Schmidt; Black and pink © istockphoto.com/blackwaterimages; Punk Girl © istockphoto.com/Kuzma; Woman escaping © Jose antonio Sanchez reyes/Photos.com; Young running man © Tatiana Belova/Photos.com; Gears clock © Jupiterimages/Photos.com; Woman portrait © Nuzza/Sutterstock; Explosions © Leigh Prather/Dreamstime.com; Landscape blueprints © Firebrandphotography/Dreamstime.com; Jump over wall © Ammentorp/Dreamstime.com; Mountains, CAN © Akadiusz Iwanicki/Dreamstime.com; Sphinx Bucegi © Adrian Nicolae/Dreamstime.com; Big mountains © Hoptrop/Dreamstime.com; Sunset mountains © Pklimenko/Dreamstime.com; Mountains lake © Jan Mika/Dreamstime.com; Blue night sky © Mack2happy/Dreamstime.com; Old writing © Empire331/Dreamstime.com; Young man © Shuen Ho Wang/Dreamstime.com; Abstract cells © Sur/Dreamstime.com; Helicopter © Evren Kalinbacak/Dreamstime.com; Aeroplane © Rgbe/Dreamstime.com; Phrenology illustration © Mcarrel/Dreamstime.com; Abstract interior © Sur/Dreamstime.com; Papyrus © Cebreros/Dreamstime.com; Blue shades © Mohamed Osama/Dreamstime.com; Blue background © Matusciac/Dreamstime.com; Sphinx and Pyramid © Dan Breckwoldt/Dreamstime.com; Blue background2 © Cammeraydave/Dreamstime.com; Abstract shapes © Lisa Mckown/Dreamstime.com; Yellow Field © Simon Greig/Dreamstime.com; Blue background3 © Sergey Skrebnev/Dreamstime.com; Blue eye © Richard Thomas/Dreamstime.com; Abstract landscape © CrazyB0frog/Dreamstime.com; Rameses II © Jose I. Soto/Dreamstime.com; Helicopter © Sculpies/Dreamstime.com; Vitruvian man © Cornelius20/Dreamstime.com; Scarab beetle © Charon/Dreamstime.com; Eye of Horus © Charon/Dreamstime.com; Handsome male portrait © DigitalHand Studio/Shutterstock.com; Teen girl © CREATISTA/Shutterstock.com; Berlin city nights © Matthias Haker 2011/Getty Images; Bradenburg Gate, Berlin © istockphoto.com/Nikada; Office skyscrapers in the sun © istockphoto.com/PPAM Picture; Sunset in Berlin © istockphoto.com/Nikada; Modern railway station in Berlin © istockphoto.com/Nikada; Treasure chest © istockphoto.com/hidesy; Kirche © istockphoto.com/nikonaft; Tunnel in old mine underground © istockphoto.com/Tomas Sereda; Alpine scenic © istockphoto.com/jethic; Bode Museum, Berlin, Germany © istockphoto.com/Matthew Lees Dixon; Part of the Berlin Wall © I-bag/Dreamstime.com; Sports car tachometer © istockphoto.com/gabyjalbert; Focus on Berlin, Germany © Joanne Zh/Dreamstime.com; Warehouse © Uatp1/Dreamstime.com; Train departure © Jeff Whyte/Dreamstime.com; Berlin urban © Emadrazo/Dreamstime.com; Berlin TV tower © Yuryz/Dreamstime.com; Berlin night © Ian Woolcock/Dreamstime.com; Mural on Berlin Wall © Larissa Dening/Dreamstime.com; Berlin Reichstag © istockphoto.com/tapuzina; II. World War © istockphoto.com/tunart; Aircraft BF-109 © istockphoto.com/Andrew_Howe; Flak Tower G, Vienna © Lucaderoma/Dreamstime.com; Old Bunker from II World War © Mirek Hejnicki/Dreamstime.com; Broken glass © Aprescindere/Dreamstime.com; Bunker © Mirek Hejnicki/Dreamstime.com.

6 5 4 3 2 1   Printed in Canada   121   14 15 16 17 18 19

MIX
Paper from
responsible sources
FSC® C004071

THE LAST
THIRTEEN

BOOK THREE

JAMES PHELAN

Scholastic Canada Ltd.

Toronto New York London Auckland Sydney
Mexico City New Delhi Hong Kong Buenos Aires

PREVIOUSLY

Sam fights off Solaris with the help of Shiva, the Enterprise Agent working for the Academy. They discover this "Solaris" is actually a rogue Agent, Stella, in disguise. Sam escapes down a train tunnel.

He flies to Egypt with his school friend, Xavier Dark, and climbs the Great Pyramid of Giza. There he accidentally finds a key in the Star of Egypt and returns to the Academy.

Sam's nightmares reveal the identity of the next of the last 13—it is Gabriella, an Italian pop star. Sam goes to Rome to meet her. After convincing her of the prophecy, they flee from Agents in a nail-biting drive through the city streets.

At the Vatican library, Gabriella finds a box from her dreams. Still pursued by Agents, they use a map from inside the box to lead them to the Pantheon. There, the real Solaris reveals himself in a deadly firefight.

Gabriella finds a disc hidden in the floor of the Pantheon. Sam and Solaris finally come face to face, and Sam manages to overpower him and takes off on a stolen motorbike.

As Sam leaves the city he is surrounded by German Guardians. Assuming they are there to protect him, Sam is stunned when they pull out weapons . . .

SAM

"**P**ull over! Now!" yelled the Guardian hanging out the van in front of Sam, a dart pistol aimed squarely at his head.

From the van on his left, someone fired a dart which glanced off the fuel tank of the scooter and Sam swerved wildly.

"OK, OK!" Sam shouted at his attackers. He eased off the Vespa's throttle and began to slow down.

So much for my rescue party . . . what do I do now?

Through the open doors of the van ahead, Sam could see it was loaded with men. To his left, the same. Sam guessed he was outnumbered at least ten to one. The Guardians, guns raised, all wore the uniform of the German Guard, the wolf insignia emblazoned shamelessly on their shoulders.

Traitors . . .

As the scooter puttered along the deserted road, Sam could tell the leader was growing impatient. The Guardian tilted his head toward his pistol, his grey eyes unblinking.

The gesture was clear: pull over—*now*—or get shot.

Whatever you do, don't let them get you into the van.

Sam looked around at the farms that stretched out in both directions as far as he could see in the pale light of daybreak. There was a forest up ahead, marked by a wall of tall pines with the road punching a shadowy path through the middle.

Sam continued his charade of trying to work out how to stop, knowing that at any moment they'd *make* him stop, with or without the scooter.

Wait, is that . . . ?

Ahead, beyond the van in front, on the road that wound around into the trees, Sam could see the dim lights of an approaching vehicle. It was a truck, a big one, heading their way.

Hope.

Sam gave the engine a little boost and then kicked the gear lever into neutral to give the impression that he was trying to come to a complete stop. The scooter coughed unhappily at the rough handling.

The leading van sped up to increase its distance in front of Sam, then came to a halt farther down the road. Two of the German Guardians piled out, dart pistols still aimed at Sam.

Sam slowly squeezed the rear brake of the scooter. It was now travelling as slow as it would go before becoming unstable and threatening to tip. Even though the experience of riding bikes with his friend Bill was a long time ago, it was helping Sam have enough control of the scooter to pretend to be in trouble now. All those afternoons playing chicken with Bill's uncle's tractor were paying off.

Playing chicken . . .

Sam looked across the empty road. About two metres down a steep embankment, a wire fence surrounding a farm was just visible in the soft light. Sam could see the oncoming truck clearly now, it was just a few seconds away from him.

Do it—go for it, Sam!

In the blink of an eye, Sam slammed into second gear, revved the engine and dropped the clutch.

VROOM!

The ambling scooter burst into life, shooting forward and to the left, swerving back into the middle of the road. Sam squeezed his eyes tight as he shot across the road in the tiny gap between the van behind and the huge truck roaring straight toward him. Its lights flashed and the horn blared loudly, the rush of air from the speeding truck almost knocking Sam off the scooter.

Blood pounding in his ears and adrenalin pumping, Sam threw a look over his shoulder and saw that both vans had taken off in hot pursuit after his surprise manoeuvre. He surged ahead, toward the sloped gravel embankment on the other side of the road, when behind him . . .

SMASH!

Sam risked another glance to see that one van had clipped the truck's semitrailer and had been violently twisted around on its side. Sam skidded to a halt to watch as the mess of metal and glass rolled and flipped, an unstoppable mechanical snowball that seemed to gather speed before ploughing into the second van. The impact propelled the vans through the air, before hitting the ground hard and shuddering to a stop on their sides. Sam heard the ear-piercing screech of the truck's brakes, could smell the burning rubber of tires locking hard. There was no movement from inside the vans.

Sam egged the scooter on, willing himself away from the danger and destruction behind him. The Vespa's engine redlined, revving as hard as it would go as he fumbled to find the right gear, the throttle fully open, picking up more speed down the embankment. He hit a bump, turning his rapid downward momentum into full flight.

"ARRRGGGGHHHHH!"

He had expected to navigate through a gate or gap in the fence. But instead, Sam found himself flying through the air at speed, headed for the waist-high wire fence. He cringed, held on tight and hoped for the best.

Sam winced as he felt the back tire hitting the top wire. The crash landing on the uneven, muddy surface rattled the teeth in Sam's head but the thump of the landing seemed to jolt the little scooter back to life. He hit the throttle again and sped across the grassy field, swerving to miss a goat that looked up, stunned, staring into Sam's eyes as he shot past.

Sam looked over his shoulder one last time. The vans were now an eerie mess of lights and steam. He could make out the tiny silhouette of the truck driver, standing with his hands on his head. An approaching car was slowing to a stop.

Sam continued onward, the going easier on the flat ground, heading for the cover of the dark forest ahead. He soon found the fence on the other side of the paddock. He followed its length until he came to an open gate.

In the forest, the ground was flat but blanketed in old pine needles and the scooter skittered wildly as Sam slowly navigated a way through the trees. His heart rate slowed a little, his head swimming with the shock of what had just happened.

Why were they trying to kidnap me? First the Egyptian Guardians, now these guys? Man, what about the others? Is everyone else safe?

Sam rode on under the protection of the dense forest for a while. He kept the road that cut through the trees in his sights, waiting to join it again a few kilometres down the track when he was sure he was safe. It was harder going here, the tires losing traction on the spongy forest floor, the canopy of the trees above shutting out the glare of the rising sun. Sam was grateful that the physical effort of keeping the scooter upright gave him little time to dwell on his narrow escape.

Without warning, a low-hanging tree branch seemed to materialize out of nowhere, whipping into his face and knocking him clean off the bike. He was flat on his back, groaning, the feathery tops of the pine trees above him spinning in circles in the sky . . .

SAM'S NIGHTMARE

I hear the honking of a horn and then a *ding ding*. There's a streetcar and cars coming right toward us—

I pull the boy backward just as the streetcar flashes by in a squeal of steel brakes. I turn to face him, puzzled. I know him, but why is he here?

"That was close!" he yells, then to the departing streetcar, "Watch where you're going next time!" He turns to me, "Thanks, man."

I spin around, trying to get my bearings. *Where are we?* I look for road signs, at the cars and their licence plates . . . and catch a glimpse of the Brandenburg Gate in the distance. I remember it from my history class last year.

I'm in Berlin.

I cough from the car fumes clustering around us and shelter my eyes from the grit thrown up from the passing traffic.

I blink away the dust.

We're alone inside a room. It looks like a lab. There are some large plastic tubs lined up on a stainless-steel counter.

"There's something here, I know it," the boy says. He rifles through them, full of anxiety and despair. "Here!" he finds a rolled piece of tracing paper and turns to me with a smile.

We're running down a corridor, the paper in my hand. We've made it . . .

I'm surrounded by darkness when there's a loud bang and rushing air flattens me as I open my mouth to scream. I'm flying through the air, heading into the light, brighter and brighter until . . . I'm blinded by the sun, hearing my screams mingle with another's. I look around and see I'm way up above the ground now, people below are small dots among the trees.

I close my eyes for the inevitable crash to earth but suddenly I'm gliding slowly.

I can fly?

I open my eyes to see the boy, grinning, "It's going to be OK, Sam," he laughs, almost hysterically.

And the boy's gone and it's just me, slipping, sliding, falling . . . and I see him. Solaris. His masked face looms into mine as I push him away. But my arms are heavy, I can't fight him off. He's laughing at me, becoming bigger and louder as I try to get away. And then the fire comes for me, flames shooting so close I can feel my body burning.

"Get away from me!" I'm shouting but my voice is whipped away by the pounding wind. I'm plummeting through the air—twisting, turning, *burning*.

No, not this way.

Please.

Despair washes over me as I fall without any hope of surviving.

I curl my body inward, making myself small, blocking out the flames and the rushing wind, and *him*, waiting for me.

I'm crashing to earth, with nothing to save me from—

Oblivion.

SAM

"**S**am?"

Sam opened his eyes to see a figure kneeling next to him, shaking him awake.

"Xavier?" Sam said, his hand flying up to the dream catcher at his throat. He tugged at it, straining for room to breathe.

"Yeah, man," Xavier replied. "We've got to get a move on, our clearance for takeoff is in ten minutes."

"Takeoff?" Sam asked, sitting up and rubbing the grogginess from his tired eyes.

"Yeah, ten minutes, so come on—we'll have to run across the tarmac to make it in time."

"We're . . . at an airport?" Sam looked around and the hustle and bustle of people and their luggage flitting by came into focus.

"Yeah . . ." Xavier said. "Sam, you OK?"

"Fine, yeah," Sam replied as he stood up, taking off the dream catcher and weighing it in his hand. Through the floor-to-ceiling windows he could see planes taxiing back and forth, a large cargo carrier taking off in the distance. He suddenly remembered the night before—Gabriella's party in Rome, the chase through the subterranean levels of the Vatican, facing Solaris and evading those treacherous German Guardians, and now . . . "Where *are* we?"

"Italy, of course."

"I mean, in what city?"

"Just outside Siena. Are you OK? You said you got hit on the head."

Hit on the head? Then, it came flooding back. Sam had woken up in the forest and ridden back up to the road far enough past the mangled vehicles to stay out of sight. A few kilometres north he stopped at a gas station and called Xavier, heading on to where Xavier said he'd pick him up and take him to . . . "Wait, where'd I say we had to go?"

"Switzerland," Xavier said. "You called me and said that you needed to get back to Switzerland as quickly as possible—that your friends would be worried about you but that their phone line was down. Are you OK to go? Our flight crew's prepped to take us there in like . . ."

He checked his watch.

"Eight minutes. We gotta hustle."

Sam looked at Xavier's watch, but his eyes were unseeing. His dream was flooding back to him—the street, the streetcar, the bustle of the crowd, and more—being in the air, the wind, the flames . . . and Xavier. The boy in the dream was *Xavier!*

"Why are you looking at me like that?" Xavier said.

"Like what?"

"Like you've just seen a ghost."

"Sorry . . . kinda the opposite, actually. About our trip to Switzerland . . ." Sam looked at his friend. "Something tells me you feel like we need to be someplace else."

Xavier stopped mid-stride.

Sam continued, "Like you might have an idea about where to go. Some other country?"

"Really? I thought that was just my imagination working overtime in my dreams," Xavier said. He hesitated, squinting at Sam. "Is this like when I dreamed of helping you outside the museum in New York?"

Sam nodded. "You know the 'secret agent' stuff I told you about . . . well, it's kind of true, but it has more to do with dreams than being James Bond. Although . . . the saving the world bit is actually part of the deal."

Xavier was, for once, speechless.

"Let's get on the plane, and I'll tell you all about it. Deal?" Sam smiled.

"O . . . kay . . ." Xavier mumbled.

"I'm sorry to rush you but we've no time to lose. You up for this?"

The world blurred past them as they stood in the open doorway to the airfield. Sam could see Xavier wrestling with himself as different emotions flickered across his face—disbelief, surprise, horror, excitement . . .

"I guess we're taking a quick detour to Berlin, then?" Xavier finally smiled.

Sam nodded again, as he slipped his dream catcher into the back of a passing cleaning cart.

"Why'd you do that?" Xavier said.

"Because," Sam said, starting to walk across the tarmac, "it's time to get off the grid. There are way too many people looking for me, and not many I can trust."

And I didn't realize until this morning just how few that would be.

EVA

"**W**e can't leave Sam," Eva said, breaking the silence. Next to her, Lora and Gabriella rode in quiet contemplation as they travelled in a three-vehicle convoy headed north, speeding toward a private airstrip near the Swiss border.

"Sam gave us the chance to escape and now we need to take these," Lora gestured to the disc, book and key that Gabriella still clutched tightly to her, "to the Academy, and the Professor," she replied. "We can't risk something so valuable falling into Solaris' hands." She looked meaningfully at Gabriella.

"But how can Sam be safe without us?" Eva objected. "You saw what it was like for all of us to come up against Solaris, let alone swarms of Enterprise Agents."

"He knows what he's doing now," Lora said. "He's smart enough to keep his head down and he'll contact us if things start to get out of control—he's not going to take on more than he can handle, not on his own."

Eva nodded but remained unconvinced. The terrifying

scenes in Rome replayed in her mind as she shivered and drew her coat tighter.

Yeah, he'll keep his head down. If someone doesn't take it clean off . . .

"I think Sam will be fine," Gabriella said in her Italian-accented English. "He was *amazing* in Roma—always a step ahead of those who chased us. And back there at the temple, what he did to save me, he's . . . he's incredible!"

Great, Eva thought, *now some pop star thinks Sam's amazing and incredible, he's bound to be safe, right?*

Eva grimaced at her and nodded.

How does she figure into all this anyway? Doesn't she have enough of a life to lead without being one of the last 13? How do you go from entertaining the world to saving it?

At the snow line in the foothills of the Italian Alps, the convoy pulled up at a small airstrip and everyone spilled out into the cold air.

"Pit stop. The plane will be ready in five minutes," Lora called out.

Eva trudged through the snow and got herself a hot chocolate from the battered machine in the hut-like lounge area and stood outside, looking absently at a wall map of the region.

Her breath fogged out in front of her. She heard footsteps behind her, scrunching in the snow.

"Would you believe, I've never been to the Alps." Gabriella mused, standing next to her.

"You're about to get a bird's eye view," Eva replied flatly. "It's pretty spectacular . . . if you're not too jaded for that kind of thing."

"Jaded?"

"Being bored of something," Eva explained. "I guess you would have seen all kinds of amazing places before."

Gabriella was silent and Eva continued to stare deliberately at the map.

"You don't like me, do you?" Gabriella asked.

Eva thought about a few replies before closing her eyes and saying, "Sam's out there, somewhere, alone and in harm's way—and he nearly got killed last night . . ."

"He nearly got killed because of *me*," Gabriella said quietly.

"I'm worried about him. I'm not blaming you, but we should be doing more to help Sam."

"OK. Thank you."

"Thank you? For what?" Eva frowned.

"For being honest," Gabriella said. "Most people do not speak to me with honesty. They see me as what was created around me. But the 'pop *principessa*' thing, it's just a mask. That's not really me. This is me—here, now. I am worried about Sam too. But only a little."

"Only a little?" Eva scoffed.

"What I know about your friend Sam is that he's very brave," Gabriella said, turning to walk toward the plane.

Eva slowly followed behind Gabriella, keeping her distance.

Well, you'll just have to excuse me if I decide to do more than just wait around to see what happens next, principessa.

SAM

"That's it," Xavier said. "It's the building from my dream."

Man, it's so lucky Xavier can remember some of his true dream from just the other night. Hmm, luck—or should that be "fate"?

"And it only took a few minutes wandering around the Brandenburg Gate to find it. Not bad, I think. Now all we have to do is find a way inside," Sam said.

They stood across the road from the nondescript brick building on the edge of Berlin's business district. The midday traffic was picking up as the lunch-hour rush set in, and the two of them looked nervously about. Everything seemed normal—in fact, everything seemed too normal, too calm, as Sam imagined sinister-looking Agents and rogue Guardians hiding just out of sight.

Agents, Guardians—everyone's after us now. What has my life turned into?

And Sam could hardly believe how well Xavier had taken the news about being a true Dreamer.

Maybe it isn't so tough to be the messenger. Gabriella

took it in her stride too . . . I didn't really get into the whole
"last 13" thing though . . . one step at a time.

For now Xavier seemed happy to go along with Sam's
assurance that they were doing something important.
He'd not pressed Sam for too many details, and Sam had
been relieved to delay that conversation.

Sam snapped back into the moment and studied the
building, which had thick steel bars over its wire-mesh
windows. It was a veritable fortress, keeping safe what was
stored within.

"I mean, having dreams come true like this . . ." Xavier said.

"Don't worry, you'll get used to it," Sam reassured him.

"It's unbelievable!"

"You can say that again," Sam said, preparing to cross
the road once there was a break in the traffic.

"It's unbeliev—"

"Come *on*," Sam said, quickly making to cross the
road—"Wait!"

He pulled Xavier back from a passing streetcar that had
appeared from behind a truck travelling the other way.

"That was close! Thanks, man," Xavier said, watching
the streetcar trundle up the street in a cloud of dust.

"That'll teach us," Sam laughed nervously.

"To cross at the lights?"

"To remember our dreams!" Sam looked left and right.
"Come on."

By the red steel door was a plaque—

ANTIKENSAMMLUNG BERLIN

BERLIN ANTIQUITIES COLLECTION
SITE 2B

"Should we knock?" Sam asked.

"I find it easier," Xavier said with a smile, twisting the handle, "when the door's unlocked, to just go on in."

They walked into a surprisingly high-tech foyer. A large glass door was set into a secondary glass wall, in front of which sat a receptionist behind a long marble desk. The young woman turned to them with an expectant look.

"What do we do now?" Xavier said, standing stock-still just inside the entrance.

"Just go talk to her," Sam said quietly out the corner of his mouth. "Tell her that your dad funded the project on the Ramses Dream Stele dig and that we were sent here to go through any remaining items." He smiled at the waiting woman. "That's got to be what we were looking at in the dream. Right?"

The receptionist continued to look at them as she

smoothed back her hair, putting down a magazine and leaning forward.

Xavier was uncharacteristically hesitant. He looked to Sam as if to say, *are you sure this will work?*

"You're Mr. Charm, so go on, *charm* her," Sam hissed.

"Going through items . . . right, good one," Xavier said as he walked up to the receptionist, Sam following close behind. Xavier placed his hands elegantly on the desk. "*Guten morgen*, Miss. I'm Xavier Dark, I'm here to inventory the—"

"Dr. Xavier Dark?" she interrupted him, eyes wide.

"Ah—*yes*, that's right," Xavier replied in a deeper voice, coughing and standing up a bit straighter. "I've financed countless exhibitions and field work for your museum. Surely you know of me?"

"Ah, yes, we've been expecting you. Forgive me, I'm new here," the receptionist said in flawless English, suddenly animated and showing them both a broad, gleaming white smile. "I'm so sorry Dr. Dark, you are here earlier than your appointed time, my apologies. And, well . . ."

"You thought I'd be older?"

What? Don't mention that!

"Yes, actually," the receptionist said with an embarrassed giggle.

"I get that a lot," Xavier said, now cool as a cucumber once more. "Good genes," Xavier said, leaning back on the desk and giving her a wink.

There was a moment's hesitation—

Uh-oh. Too much?

And then, "But, of course. Just a moment," she said as she brought up a screen on her computer.

Xavier turned around to Sam and grinned. Sam rolled his eyes but smiled back.

Yes, yes, you're very charming . . .

"If you have some ID, please?" the receptionist asked. "Just a formality for you, Dr. Dark, but we must follow procedure."

Without missing a beat, Xavier flashed his passport fast enough to stop her from noticing his date of birth.

UNITED STATES OF AMERICA

PASSPORT
PASSEPORT
PASAPORTE

USA

Type/Type/Tipo   Code/Code/Codigo   Passport No./No du Passeport/No de Pasaporte
P   USA   D91573515

Surname / Nom / Apellidos
DARK III

Given Names / Prenoms / Nombres
XAVIER CHRISTIAN

Nationality / Nationalite / Nacionalidad
UNITED STATES OF AMERICA

Date of birth / Date de naissance / Fecha de nacimiento
07 Aug 1998

Place of birth / Lieu de naissance / Lugar de nacimiento
SEATTLE, U.S.A.

Sex/Sexe/Sexo
M

Date of issue / Date de delivrance / Fecha de expedicion
16 Feb 2012

Authority/Autorite/Autoridad
United States
Department of State

Date of expiration / Date d'expiration / Fecha de caducidad
16 Feb 2022

Endorsements / Mentions Speciales / Anotaciones
SEE PAGE 27

USA

P<USADARK<<XAVIERCHRISTIAN<<<<<<<<<<<<<<<<<<
D91573515<9USA6813745 9M8492761<<<<<<<<<<<<13

A nearby guard stepped up and handed over two visitor badges.

"Down the corridor, third door on the right, and I'll have someone from the Pergamon's research department attend to you right away," the receptionist said apologetically. "As I mentioned, you are earlier than expected, otherwise they would be waiting here for you, sir. Our apologies."

"Thank you," Xavier said, perfectly playing the part of his father. "We will wait there for your researcher, third door on the right."

The receptionist nodded and pressed a hidden button. The heavy glass door clicked open and she motioned them through. Near the third door on the right, the corridor deserted, Xavier turned to Sam.

"I can't believe she thinks I'm my father," he said with a cheeky grin.

"That's a lucky break for us," Sam said. "Good thing you can pass for a guy with a Ph.D."

"But that means that my father's due here later today," Xavier said.

"I guess he might have made the appointment a while back, to go through what's left from the dig site where they found the Dream Stele," Sam said.

"Yeah, that could be right," Xavier said. "And he'd especially want to come now—to see what's left after the Stele was destroyed in New York."

"Well, there's only one way to find out," Sam said,

"which is to see what's behind this door . . ."

". . . and to find out if the rest of my dream comes true," Xavier finished Sam's thought. Sam noticed Xavier warily joining the dots, matching up his dream of coming here to the reality of what was actually unfolding.

"I'm having the weirdest sense of déjà vu, being here with you right now, doing something we've done before in my dream. It's beyond spooky," he added.

"This is how it feels to live out your dream in waking life. You'll get used to it," Sam replied, giving Xavier a reassuring nudge.

"Yeah," Xavier said. "And there *is* something here, I know it . . . but what will we tell my dad?"

"Was your father in your dream?" Sam asked.

"I think so, but not here," Xavier said. "I can't be sure though, it's confusing."

"We'll worry about what to say to him if and when we end up seeing him," Sam replied. "Come on, let's find what we came for and then get out of here, OK?"

"But . . ."

"What?"

"I just remembered more of my dream," Xavier replied, "I don't think we get out so easily."

"Oh?" Sam said, his own dream playing back in his mind's eye.

"Yeah, it went really . . . crazy."

"Crazy how? Can you remember anything specific?"

Sam said, his hand on the door handle. Going through Xavier's dream together on the flight to Berlin, he'd thought they knew enough to manage this part without too many complications. They'd arrive at the archives, get into the room, find a scroll that was somehow important and run before they were discovered.

"No, it's so frustrating. I'm just getting flashes of it. I can see boots . . . someone's boots," Xavier looked at Sam.

"Well, the best thing we can do now is get in and out as quick as we can."

"Yeah."

Sam opened the door.

ALEX

Alex stretched his arms above his head and cracked his knuckles as he swung around in his chair to face Shiva. His new boss was seated next to him, preoccupied with the code scrolling across the large screens ranged along his desk. He sensed Alex's gaze and tore his eyes away from the glare, pulling out his earphones. Alex could hear heavy metal music pounding away in them.

"How you doing, Alex? Need a break?" Shiva said. "Let's grab a drink." He rose from his chair.

"Sure thing." Alex followed him out of the dimly lit computer lab, passing in front of Matrix, who scowled at Alex as they walked by. "What's his problem, anyway?" Alex asked when they were out of earshot. "How come we never hear about what he's working on?"

"That's just his baseline for friendliness, don't worry about it," Shiva laughed. "And he's always been a bit secretive and weird. Part of his genius charm, I guess. But how are you finding the work? Not too challenging for you?" he laughed again.

"As if!" Alex shot back with a smirk. "Actually, I'm kinda loving it. Feels like I'm really in the game now, trying to predict who the last 13 might be."

"And you know we have other techs working on how to find Solaris," Shiva said. "Stopping him and finding the last 13 are the two best ways we have of getting the situation under control and making sure no one else gets hurt."

They walked back from the drinks machine, quietly slurping as they went.

"So you really believe we can find some of the last 13?" Alex asked.

"Well, Sam was an Enterprise Dreamer so there's every reason to hope we might have successfully created more of them. And that code we're working on is just one way we're trying to narrow it down to the most likely candidates."

Alex sat back at his desk and returned to his screens.

Saving the world, one line of code at a time. This'll do for now.

Shiva threw a scrunched-up paper ball at Alex. When Alex looked up, Shiva was pointing to the door.

Alex's mom, Phoebe, stood in the doorway. "You wanted to know if we had any updates on Sam?" Phoebe said, coming over to sit beside him at his desk.

"And?" Alex replied, immediately looking to her. "Is he OK?"

"It seems that he's fine," Phoebe replied. "He popped up on the grid north of Rome."

"Was he alone?"

"I'm not sure, that's all I learned in the briefing," Phoebe said.

"Where's he headed?" Alex said.

"He was on a private jet to Germany," Phoebe said.

"Can I contact him?" Alex asked.

"I'm not sure if that's a good idea," Phoebe said. "Not just yet. It would raise questions around here. Too many questions, which we're not sure yet how we want to answer."

"But—I'm a part of this dreaming thing, you said so yourself, the Director too. I mean, I could be one of the last 13, like Sam, right?" Alex said.

"We don't know yet, but of course it's possible," Phoebe said. She looked away as she added, "I'm not sure I'd want you to be. If something happened to you . . ."

Alex nodded and looked down at his desk. "I know, Mom, it's OK. I just wish I knew one way or the other. It's the not knowing that's really messing with my head. When do *you* think I'll know?"

"If that could be foreseen, or designed somehow, then this would all be so much easier," she said. "That's why Jack has you all working so hard on figuring that out."

"But until then it's all up to chance?"

"Chance, destiny . . . something like that," she smiled.

SAM

"**W**hat the . . . ?"

The room was about a hundred times bigger than Sam had anticipated.

This isn't the lab from my dream. Guess we're not there yet.

Steel shelves reached a ceiling over five metres above them and stretched out in long rows, nearly as far as the eye could see as they disappeared into the gloom. Sam closed the door behind them. It clunked shut with a heavy thud.

"Great," Xavier said. "We've got a warehouse of stored junk to go through. We'll be here for days before we find this scroll. I thought someone was coming to meet us? Where do we start?"

"It was your dream, buddy," Sam replied. "Think back."

"You dreamed it too," Xavier said.

"Not the finer details like you did. My dream jumped around from the moment I opened the door. We need more info."

"Right, ah . . ." Xavier closed his eyes and squeezed them

tight as he tried to recall his dream. Then he opened them and shrugged. "Nope—you know what? I got nothing. Nada. Zilch. Maybe the dream fried my brain."

"Then let's start to look around," Sam said. "Maybe you'll see something that'll jog your memory."

"Right, OK, cool. Which way?" Xavier asked.

"Straight?" Sam suggested.

"Really? I was thinking left."

"Right," Sam said. "It's your dream, we'll go left."

"Or right," Xavier said. "I mean—do you feel that maybe right is the better way to go?"

"Why?" Sam said.

"You said right," Xavier replied.

"When?" Sam asked.

"A couple of seconds ago."

"Huh?"

"Oh man . . ." Xavier rubbed his hands through his hair in frustration and confusion.

"Xav, I think it's up to you—" Sam began.

"Or we can totally go straight," Xavier said. "I mean, first you said straight, like immediately you said it, so that might be right, yeah?"

Sam shook his head and rubbed his temples as a headache set in.

"Can I help you?"

"Argh!" Sam nearly jumped out of his skin as a woman appeared behind him.

"Wow, where'd you come from?" he gasped.

"This is a restricted area," she said in clipped, crisp tones. Dressed in a lab coat and carrying an electronic pad, she seemed suspicious of the two visitors before her and she leaned forward to scrutinize their visitor passes. "I see your passes grant you access. But you were discussing where to go?"

They took a long look at each other.

"This is Dr. Xavier Dark," Sam said, jumping into the silence and motioning to Xavier. "And I am his assistant, Dr. Samuel Gold-en—Goldenstein. Professor, actually. I've got two Ph.D.'s, actually. Isn't that right, Dr. Dark?"

Sam smiled to Xavier who looked as though they'd been found out as frauds and would be frogmarched out to waiting police.

"A little young for doctors, aren't you?" the woman asked, one eyebrow arched over her glasses.

"American colleges," Sam explained with a wave of the hand. "You can buy any degree for a price these days." He nudged Xavier with his elbow. *What's wrong with him? Is he afraid of getting into trouble with his father?*

"Hmm, so I've heard . . ." she said, consulting her pad. "Dr. Dark, I see. You are here about the artifacts from the Larnaca site?"

"Yes!" Xavier snapped back to life, perhaps a little too enthusiastically. "Ah, that is correct, yes, the artifacts from the Larnaca site. Excellent. Professor Goldenbloom?"

Sam coughed back a laugh. "We'd like to personally inventory what is left here," he added. "From the site. At Larnar . . ."

"Larnaca," she said, her eyes narrowing. "Very well, follow me."

"Larnaca, right," Sam said, walking next to her. "I like your accent. German?"

She gave Sam a withering look and turned to Xavier. "And everything is well with the exhibition in New York?" she asked as they crossed the labyrinthine corridors of storage.

"Oh yes, why wouldn't they be?" Xavier replied.

"I read a news report about the opening night," she countered. "That some pieces may have been damaged?"

"Hmm," Xavier said, looking to Sam. "A minor embarrassment, someone smoking in the toilets set off the sprinklers, but everything's fine—"

"I heard from a reliable source that there was a fire," she said.

"A very small fire, nothing to worry about," Sam added. "More a smouldering hand towel really, right, Doctor?"

"Yes, I do believe you are right, Professor," Xavier replied.

"Another example of American laxness with works of historical significance," she replied, shaking her head. "Perhaps it is because you Americans are so gung-ho and careless, and have no concept of real history."

"And what," Sam said, "something like that would never happen in Germany?"

She stopped walking and turned to faced them. "No."

"Well, we'd love to chat more, but . . ." Xavier said, his voice finding some authority. "My collection?"

Sam looked to Xavier who shrugged. Both knew that the charade was crumbling—they had to see what was left and get out while they still could.

"It's here," she said, tapping away at her tablet computer.

"Let's get on then, shall we?"

"Americans . . ." she muttered. "Always in a hurry."

An electronic whirring noise erupted out of the gloom high above, followed by hydraulic sounds, and then an ever-increasing whine as a robotic lift came down to their level, loaded with several plastic containers, each the size of a large crate.

"Here they are," she said. "We can follow the lifter to the viewing room, where you can inventory what remains of the excavation that you financed, *Dr. Dark*."

"Er, excellent," Xavier said, faltering in her scathing gaze. "Thank you, Fräulein."

They fell into step behind the archivist and her robotic crane, walking in silence. Sam hoped they'd find what they needed and hoped they'd find it in time.

EVA

"**S**am's just popped up," Lora said as she ended her call and turned around to the girls who were looking out the plane windows at the spectacular mountains below.

"Where?" Eva asked.

"Berlin. His face came up on the city's security cameras and Jedi got a match through his computer system," Lora said, tapping on her phone screen again. "It's odd though, his dream catcher is stationary—in Italy."

"Is he OK?"

"Jedi said he looked fine."

"Berlin—how'd Sam get there so fast?" Eva said.

"Well, judging by where he's left his dream catcher," Lora said, frowning, "I'm guessing he caught a flight from an airstrip near Siena."

"What's in Berlin?" Gabriella asked.

"He'll be following his next dream," Lora said.

Eva said, "Without help?"

Lora shook her head. "Jedi said he was with his friend,

Xavier Dark."

"I wonder why he's with Xavier again?" Eva said. "I guess that's how he got his ride to Germany . . ."

"I suspect so," Lora said, then, noticing Gabriella's vacant expression, asked, "Are you all right?"

Gabriella nodded and pointed out the small plane window. "Look how beautiful the world is . . . it's so easy to forget, to just not notice," she said slowly, gazing out across the seemingly endless mountains. "The world looks different now—more precious . . . knowing that it is in danger, that we're fighting for it, no?"

"Can't you call him?" Eva asked Lora, bringing the conversation back to Sam.

"I tried, but his phone's been off. What's more worrying," Lora said, "is that the German Guardians have defected too. So we don't even have anyone locally who can get there quickly if he needs help. We don't have many people left we can trust to protect him."

Gabriella turned to look at them both, her face now as serious as theirs.

The mountain campus of the Academy never failed to impress Eva. She resisted the urge to press her nose against the window of the light plane as it touched down on the short runway and came to a stop outside the main building.

But she did laugh at Gabriella's horrified expression at their abrupt landing on the tiny airstrip, remembering how she'd felt the first time arriving here.

"It was a monastery, yes?" Gabriella said, climbing out behind Lora and Eva.

"It was, once," Lora said, ushering them inside and out of the billowing high-altitude winds that whipped ice and snow in a vertical assault.

Eva dusted the snow out of her short dark hair and followed Lora. They passed a group of students, who smiled nervously at them. It was only days ago they had lost two of their teachers, Sebastian and Tobias, and also Alex. *They're probably thinking about who hasn't come back.*

"I'll let the Professor know we're here, and show him these," Lora said to Eva and Gabriella, holding the brass disc, the book and key. "I'm sure he'll want to speak with you once you've rested. Eva, Gabriella can bunk with you, and then I'll see you both later."

"Sure, whatever . . ." Eva said, feeling all talked-out. She was so tired. She just wanted a bed, any bed—now.

"Share the room?" asked Gabriella, stopping in the corridor.

"Yes," said Lora, "all the students here at the Academy share with someone else. Especially in the current circumstances."

"Or perhaps I could stay in a hotel, close by? I can visit here when you need me, yes?" Gabriella said.

"There *is* no hotel near here," Lora said. "Besides, you wouldn't be safe. You need to be here, you are one of the last 13—your involvement in the rest of this race could be vital."

"But I have had my dream, we already found the piece from the Pantheon and I don't know anything else. I don't even understand what it is for," Gabriella said, confused.

"Yes, that's all true," said Lora, sympathetically, "but we still aren't certain what lies ahead, for any of us. For now, we need to stick together. Look—go with Eva, get some rest. We can discuss it more with the Professor."

Lora smiled at them before turning and walking through a doorway off the main corridor, leaving Eva and Gabriella staring at each other.

"Well, I guess you'd better follow me," Eva said. "This way." She led Gabriella down the hallway in the direction of her dorm wing. Gabriella looked around with curiosity as they passed the dining hall and study rooms. Their silent journey was accompanied by stares, whispers and even some squeals from the other students—Gabriella's arrival was not going unnoticed. Some looked starstruck to see the pop idol among them. Gabriella waved and flashed her megawatt smile at everyone. By the time they had reached the rec room near the dorm, a huge group of kids were trailing them, calling out to Gabriella.

"Well, that didn't take long," Eva murmured to herself.

Gabriella stopped to meet her fans, signing autographs

in a frenzy. Flashes of light from phone cameras popped continuously, and Gabriella posed for photograph after photograph.

She doesn't even look tired—or like she's been battling Solaris half the night.

"Thank you! Thank you, everyone. *Grazie!*" Gabriella said, finally. "I'll see you all again soon." She blew kisses in the air and made her way back to Eva. Eva took this as her cue to continue to lead the way to what was now *their* room.

"It's not your usual five-star hotel," Eva said, as they entered the room, closing the door behind them.

"No . . . it is a change from the Ritz, for sure," Gabriella smiled.

"I know it's not glamorous, but the people here are pretty amazing," Eva replied, hearing the defensiveness in her voice, before adding, "and you're not on a red carpet now. You don't have to act like that for them."

"That's normal for me," Gabriella retorted.

"Yeah, well," Eva said, collapsing on her bed, "I don't think there is a normal for anyone anymore."

SAM

"So, why is this called the Larnaca find?" Sam asked Xavier. A minute ago, the woman had left them alone with the container in a lab—the room they had both dreamed about.

"Larnaca is a city in Cyprus," Xavier said. "It's an island in the Mediterranean," he continued, seeing the blank look on Sam's face. "Seriously, did you never listen in geography class? No, wait, that's because you used to sit with what's her name—what *was* her name? The pretty blond girl, with the braces . . ."

"I listened in class," Sam replied, ignoring the jibe. "Guess the difference is that I never had my dad's jet plane to go flying around the globe proving Newton's third law of motion."

"First law," Xavier said. "Geez, you still thinking about that science class?"

"It's kinda burned in my memory," Sam said. "Seeing as that's the day I was plucked from school at gunpoint and all that."

"This was from the dig site!" Xavier interrupted, pulling out the contents of the plastic tubs lined up on the stainless-steel counter. He rifled through them, suddenly full of anxiety. "It must be here, I know it."

"We both saw the scroll, we've just got to find it," Sam said, looking through all the documents recording the archaeological dig.

Xavier stopped his rummaging and looked at Sam and said, "Look for tracing paper, a big sheet with a wax rubbing on it."

"A rubbing of . . ."

"Hieroglyphs. You'll know it when you see it."

They pulled smaller boxes out onto the table and looked at the inventory sheets affixed to each lid.

"Sixteenth century pottery fragments," Xavier said, reading off the first one.

"Unknown organic matter," Sam said, reading off a lid. He looked inside—it looked like bits of rocks and debris.

"Animal bones," Xavier said. "Gross."

They went through the tubs systematically, sorting through stacks of documents, and little plastic bags and containers filled with old coins.

"So tell me more about Larnaca . . ." Sam said.

"Right. Well, from what I remember, my father had an archaeological team, overseen by Ahmed, excavating there," Xavier said, "specifically at Larnaca Castle. They identified an area where no previous archaeological work had been carried out. They found an underground vault where artifacts had been buried five hundred years before."

"How old is the castle?" Sam asked.

"Much older than that," Xavier said.

"So someone buried this ancient Egyptian stuff there around 1500?" Sam said. "The bottom half of Ramses' Dream Stele, and the Star of Egypt, which we now know was really made by da Vinci," Sam said, "and contained his key." He looked at Xavier.

"Maybe explain the whole story to me later, huh? Let's keep looking," Xavier said.

"Hmm," Sam said, scanning over several other tubs with similar contents, then, "Here's something—*recordings from site.*"

Xavier opened the box and saw stacks of notes and papers, depicting grid diagrams of the excavations carried out and journal entries. "Here!" Xavier pulled out a rolled piece of tracing paper and they cleared the bench to lay it out. "I *knew* Ahmed would have done this! He taught me to do these as a kid. Wow, this is so cool."

I've seen this before! At least the top half of it.

"This is it!" Sam said, marvelling at the detailed wax rubbing of the Dream Stele. "It matches what I saw at the Academy—it's the missing half, the piece that the rogue Guardians destroyed in New York! I thought your father said that no one had seen the broken half of the Dream Stele?"

"That's just what he said at the museum—that's my dad, a showman to the last . . ." Xavier said. "The researchers would have checked over everything that was sent to New York, probably planning to do 3-D laser scans after the artifacts were revealed to the public."

"Well, they can't do that to the Dream Stele now. Or the Star of Egypt." Sam instinctively reached for the key that hung under his shirt. But it was gone, given to Gabriella for safekeeping. *A long way from here. A long way from danger.*

Sam swallowed hard. *I wonder how they're all doing. I hope they're safe back at the Academy now.*

"I can't believe I forgot to ask, but have you heard from Dr. Kader?" Sam said.

"Nothing so far . . . but listen, let's take this and—" Xavier interrupted Sam's reverie but stopped short as he heard footsteps echoing along the concrete floor outside. Whoever was coming was headed there in a hurry.

We've taken too long . . . Xavier's dream is coming true!

ALEX

Alex watched Stella, the operations director for the Enterprise, as she took her team of Agents through a training drill. He sat in a glass-fronted observation room overlooking the mock battlefield below, which was really a two-storey warehouse, the size of three basketball courts. Several small structures were set up as houses or offices, and there were a couple of fake parked cars and a few big wooden boxes for defensive positions.

It was a paintball shootout minus the paint. In the dim light of the black-painted landscape below, he could make out two teams with twelve Agents on each side. Stella led one group, a large guy called Henk led the other. Their objective seemed to be to get whatever was in the centre building, which looked like a little wood house. Their weapons were laser guns, which recorded hits on their full-body armour.

Alex leaned forward and watched the tactics play out below.

Stella moved her team first, and they moved *fast*. She

split them into three smaller teams, silently motioning for two teams to wrap around the opposite sides of the room in a pincer movement, suppressing the other force. Their middle team, with Stella leading, surged forward for the prize. In reach of the target building, the opposition had split into two and made their big defensive move, pushing outward with all their personnel at once. The ensuing battle was fairly even, with half the advancing team down and the remainder pulling back to cover.

After that skirmish, Stella's two side-teams were down to two Agents each, the "dead" ones having to walk back to the start lines with their laser weapons held above their heads.

What happened next was so quick he almost missed it—those two teams of two each began to fire on their opposite numbers, forcing them to remain in cover positions and keep their heads down, while Stella and her group of four rushed for the house. One of the other team, Henk perhaps, broke free and ran to a cover spot behind a vehicle, and that's when Stella's final team split again: two rushed the breakaway guy, running out in the open to flush him out as if their lives were expendable so long as Stella won.

And win she did. She rushed to the house and the lights went up, signifying the end of the exercise. Alex watched as Stella exited, smiling and victorious. She did not bother to thank her team and shouted at the "dead" men who'd made stupid mistakes. Then she walked from the room alone, leaving the Agents to regain their battered pride and talk through their mistakes.

Alex learned one thing that he'd already suspected—*I wouldn't want to come up against Stella in a fight.*

SAM

"**W**here can we hide?" Xavier whispered as the foot-falls outside neared the door.

"Here, quick!" Sam pointed to a long steel cupboard tucked under a bench set into the wall. It was a tight squeeze and Xavier's elbow pushed into Sam's nose, which was pressed up to the crack between the doors. The sound of the paper crinkling in Sam's grasp echoed inside the steel confines of their hideout. The lab door was flung open and five pairs of boots marched in.

"Can you see anything?" Xavier whispered.

"Only your elbow!" Sam replied.

"Sorry." Xavier shifted slightly.

"Quiet!" Sam muttered.

There was near-silent shuffling as they shifted positions. Through the small slit between the doors Sam peered out and saw a group of men walk over to the large open containers. Sam glimpsed their unmistakable uniform as they went past their hiding spot.

The German Guardians . . . of course.

A big guy had his back to them, along with the woman who'd shown them into the room. Three others remained near the wall, but were swiftly ordered with a couple of hand motions to search other rooms.

Maybe if we stay in here, and stay quiet . . .

Sam's sweaty hand slipped on the steel under him and poked Xavier who let out a little yelp.

They fell silent. Sam swallowed hard and put his eye back to the crack between the doors.

Their commotion hadn't gone unnoticed.

The big guy turned around and Sam recognized his face. It was definitely one of the German Guardians. He'd seen him in one of the vans—he'd fired the dart at Sam's scooter. And now here he was, with the same idea that Sam and Xavier had—to gather any remaining trace left of the Dream Stele. Only this guy would want to . . . what, destroy it? Take it to whoever he was working for? Either way, Sam couldn't let that happen.

Sam watched as the guy cautiously walked toward their cabinet.

"You trust me, right?" Sam whispered to Xavier.

"Trust you?" Xavier asked.

"Count of three, we jump out. I'll grab his legs and try to bring him down, you go for his gun."

"How come I'm the one going for a weapon?" Xavier said.

"One, two—"

The cupboard doors flew open.

"ARGH!" Sam lunged head first and took the Guardian by surprise. That was all he had—surprise. He managed to knock him off his feet and pin him to the ground.

"Xavier!" Sam yelled. *"Now!"*

But Xavier was not right behind him as planned. The Guardian was struggling to catch his breath and sat up, bringing his hands up toward Sam's throat

Sam flipped backward off the Guardian and the two of them leapt to their feet, ready to fight.

"Eat this!" Xavier said, pulling an object from his backpack. There was a *BANG!* and sparks flew.

The Guardian convulsed and stumbled back in surprise and unwilling compliance. Xavier had shot the Guardian square in the chest with a taser, the two probes sticking out of his chest, fine wires flexing as Xavier applied more juice and the Guardian collapsed to the ground, unconscious.

"Wow," Xavier said. "I've always wanted to try that," he grinned.

"Let's go," Sam said, gathering up the rest of their belongings and slinging his backpack over his shoulder, the rubbing of the Dream Stele safely tucked into a side pocket.

The archivist stood rooted to the spot in shock. When Sam turned to her, she backed away, throwing her hands up in front of her face.

"Please—" she stammered.

"Where's the closest fire escape?" Sam asked as non-threateningly as he could manage.

She pointed down the hall.

"Thanks," Sam said, taking the Guardian's dart gun from a holster under his suit jacket and forcing himself to get the other, deadlier gun out of another holster. He pulled the magazine out and threw it across the room, following Xavier out the door.

"So," Xavier said, falling into step beside Sam as they ran. "The count of three, huh? Next time, let's just charge right ahead."

"Deal. And that was some nice backup," Sam said as they turned at the exit sign and saw the fire door dead ahead. "Where'd you get a taser?"

"After Ahmed went missing, and all the crazy things that seemed to be happening, I thought I should pick one up," Xavier grimaced.

"Pick one up?" Sam said. "Like, at the mall. Like, 'Hey, I'm going out to get an ice cream. You want anything? Drink? Taser? Attack helicopter?'"

"Maybe a tank?" Xavier laughed. "Yeah, well, I guess my family's money does make some things a little easier to buy."

"Must be pretty handy having all the money in the world," Sam said as he pushed on the bar that opened the fire door. "I mean, having a rich dad and all."

As they stepped outside into the side street, Sam and Xavier came face-to-chest with a mountain of a man in a suit, standing by a massive black Mercedes. The rear door of the car opened—

And Xavier's father stepped out.

"Well, well . . ." Dr. Dark said, "seems like you boys have some explaining to do."

"It's not what you think . . . I swear . . ." Xavier began rambling at his father as Sam muscled a dumpster in front of the fire escape door and locked its wheels.

"Xavier, be quiet a moment," Dr. Dark said, then looked at Sam. "Sam . . . what's going on here?"

"I'm sorry, Dr. Dark, I know it's a big shock to find us here but we don't have time for this," Sam said quickly. "Please believe me when I say we are in danger and we have to go, right now."

There was heavy pounding at the door.

Dr. Dark saw the look of fear in Sam's eyes.

"They're like the guys who blew up the Dream Stele," Sam said. "They're after us, and one of them's gonna be real angry."

Dr. Dark nodded, and stepped back into his car as Xavier and Sam threw themselves in behind him. The chauffeur didn't need to be told to hit the pedal—the huge Mercedes took off in a haze of burnt rubber, engine roaring.

"How many were there?" Dr. Dark asked as the three of them looked out of the back window and saw the German Guardians pouring out into the alleyway.

"Duck!" Sam yelled.

SMASH!

The back window of their car was cobwebbed with cracks as a bullet hit it square in the middle.

Bullet-proof glass? Why would Dr. Dark have that?

Behind them, Guardians were climbing into a couple of white BMW sedans, obviously parked in the side street for a quick getaway.

"I sure hope your guy knows some fancy driving . . ." Sam said.

"Arnold," Dr. Dark said, his voice even and calm. "Please show our pursuers why you're the best driver in the business."

A volley of gunfire from down the alleyway tore into the brick building to their left as Arnold took the Mercedes into a big sweeping turn onto a main road.

"Take us to Hans," Dr. Dark said, Xavier and Sam scanning behind to check on the Guardians' progress.

Arnold wove the powerful car through heavy traffic, taking hazardous high-speed turns that had them all hanging onto their seats, then deftly turned onto a link road that would lead to an autobahn headed out of Berlin.

"Who's Hans?" Sam said, as they turned onto the freeway.

"He's an old acquaintance with a private estate not too far out of town," Dr. Dark said. "We won't be disturbed there."

Sam nodded.

"So," Xavier's father said as the car picked up pace on the freeway. "I think it's time you two told me what's going on and why someone just tried to kill us."

12

ALEX

Alex found Phoebe giving a seminar in a large, airy lecture room and slipped into the back to watch.

"Every person has the potential to be an Einstein," she was saying. "There is nothing that special about being exceptionally gifted. We can claim that everything that we have been told about genetics, talent and intelligence is wrong. How?"

She brought up some images on a large screen behind her.

"What processes make certain people so good at some activities? An area of research called 'expertise studies' is trying to determine the ingredients of greatness."

Several pictures of sports stars flitted across the screen.

"A great deal of practice—hours, hours and hours . . ." several of the staff laughed. "But if you look very carefully at those who end up being the best, you discover that they practise more, and *better*, than those who achieve less."

Phoebe flicked through some more images as examples.

"That is a theme that extends to all achievements.

5555555555555555555

There is a difference in how much practice and the kind of practice undertaken by the absolute legends, say in basketball—" the room cheered as a clip showed Michael Jordan leaping through the air, "—and the mere greats. The supreme achievers work hard at being great. It isn't bestowed at birth."

She brought up a portrait of Mozart.

"Most people look at child geniuses and believe that their gifts had to be the result of lucky genes. Presumably most of you agree?"

The assembled nodded.

"Every piece of evidence we have about how genes work, how brains work, where musicality actually comes from, is consistent with the idea that there is nothing that mysterious about Mozart. I am not trying to diminish his achievements, of course. But the more you look at his life, or the life of any other genius, the more you realize that this was a *process*. He reacted to an environment that was almost uniquely perfect for moulding him into a child star."

Phoebe brought up an image of a current teen pop star with his jeans hanging below his butt—and a long mathematical equation showing how sometime in the near future he'd be found out to be a talentless disaster. This time the room erupted in laughter.

"The myth of Mozart's innate talent persists because people jumble together different facts about his life," Phoebe said. "We *know* that he was interested in composing early on, and we *know* he was a remarkable performer. The untrained mind reacts by concluding he was born that way. Every time we are confronted with astonishing talent, we say it must be in the genes, because we cannot think of any other explanation. In fact, in the case of Mozart, it is clear his upbringing was also remarkable in terms of stimulating his abilities—his abilities in the waking *and* dreaming world."

Alex felt a surprising rush of pride as he listened to his mother speak, the audience focused on her every word.

I never really knew who she was before now.

"The more we read about new genes being discovered to explain human characteristics, the more our belief in the power of genes gets stronger," Phoebe continued. "Yet the vast majority of geneticists, our good Director among them—" he nodded from where he sat in the front row, "— would not want that to happen without due examination. Isn't that so?"

"Well," the Director said. "You say Mozart's greatness was not purely inborn but due to his *drive*. He practised at playing and composing better than anyone else, right? But who is to say that his drive was not inherited? The source of his greatness would still lie in his genes in that case."

"We know there are genes that influence drive," Phoebe said. "But I do not think that it is a completely natural characteristic. It becomes part of our personality and psychology and all of that is developed. Resilience and motivation can appear at different stages in people's lives and often appear in response to difficult situations. I see it as a developed trait—but I know we could argue that point all day!"

"So," the Director asked her, "do you think genetics research is going to provide us with more data that suggests that genius, that our Dreamer Gene, can be acquired as well as inherited?"

"As you know," Phoebe said, "our studies are only just beginning to figure out how the world around us affects the way genes work."

"Genes are constantly activated and deactivated by things like nutrition, hormones, nerve impulses and a host of other genes," the Director added.

"Right," Phoebe said. "It's no surprise that Dreamers most commonly activate in their teens—the genes are there at birth, but it's the constant interaction between the outside world *and* our DNA that make that magic happen. Adolescence is the time when these gifts become realized."

"In other words," the Director said, "our genes do not place a limit on our potential."

"Exactly. Our genes influence our lives, but our lives also influence our genes. We need to do a lot more to encourage that human talent, then we will *all* benefit. These things take resources, of course. But the overall message is clear. Our problem is not that our genes are inadequate, but that we have an inability, so far, to tap into what is already there. Thank you."

Applause echoed through the room.

"Well," the Director said, standing. "Few of us know our true limits and the vast majority of us have not even come close to tapping into what scientists call our 'unactualized potential.' Phoebe, you've made a compelling case for why we need both the work of the Enterprise and that of the Academy to long continue. It's nature *and* nurture, and we're on the right path. The important thing is not to get lost along the way . . . especially in these exciting times."

Alex could not make out the expression on the Director's face from where he sat, but the reference to the last 13 race was clear. As people filed out behind him, Alex sat for a moment, thinking about the odd feelings he'd had throughout his childhood, of being just that little bit different from everyone around him.

Is that something inside me or have the Enterprise and my mother been bringing me up in a certain way to make that happen? Or maybe it's both?

As Phoebe came toward him, he wondered when he would finally have an answer to whether he really could dream true dreams, and if, in the end, he really was one of the last 13.

13

SAM

It was by far the fastest that Sam had ever travelled on a road. They flashed by a police car and it didn't even bother with them. *The autobahn's cool . . .*

As Sam and Xavier relayed their story to Dr. Dark, from the exhibition in New York to their escapades in Egypt and Italy to their arrival in Germany, he nodded and accepted it all without so much as a raised eyebrow.

Sam reminded himself how he'd been seeing Dr. Dark for about three years—as his psychiatrist, sitting in weekly sessions where they'd discuss Sam's dreams and nightmares, which had been so vivid and ever more troubling over that time. Sam had thought of Dr. Dark as always being such a good listener, and it seemed that it was a trait not confined to his office.

It felt good to talk it all through like that.

"And those men shooting at us back there?" Dr. Dark said. "They are the ones who set off the explosives at the museum?"

"I'm not sure, but I think so," Sam said. "At least, they're also Guardians who have turned on the Academy. Those ones back there were German Guardians. The ones in New York were Egyptian."

Dr. Dark nodded.

Is he going to ask any more questions?

Xavier told his father how he'd tasered the guy back at the museum storage site, and Dr. Dark smiled.

"Better you tasered him than the other way around," Dr. Dark said. "And Sam, you say these Guardians work for the Academy?"

"Yes. Well, they did," Sam said. He watched for a reaction, some kind of confusion perhaps, but Dr. Dark just nodded. There was no anger, no surprise, he just took the news in. "They—the Guardians—are supposed to protect us."

Dr. Dark laughed.

"What?" Sam said. "I don't understand, you don't seem very surprised by what we're saying."

Dr. Dark smiled and chuckled to himself. "It's OK, Sam, I have every confidence in you both," he said. "I'm just glad to be with you boys now—although you're both prepared for this, perhaps more than you know."

"Thanks, Dad . . ." Xavier eventually managed. "I mean— our lives kind of changed with those gunshots back there, didn't they?"

Dr. Dark chuckled. "True."

Sam looked behind and saw no one in pursuit, none of the white BMW sedans. *Maybe they're still looking for us in Berlin.*

"There has long been . . ." Dr. Dark trailed off, looking at his son, then to Sam. "Sam, I take it that you have been to the Academy's mountain campus?"

"Yes." Sam was shocked that Dr. Dark knew of it.

"Dad . . . what's going on?" Xavier said.

"It's hard to know where to begin," Dr. Dark paused for a moment, then said, "Sam, you would have learned about the Council of Dreamers at the Academy?"

Sam gave up completely on being surprised anymore. Clearly Dr. Dark was more than just a psychiatrist for teenagers with bad dreams. Xavier had turned pale with anticipation.

"A little," Sam said. "I mean I've heard about them, the Professor was going to Paris to talk to them about everything that's going on."

"The Council of Dreamers has been in existence in some form for centuries," Dr. Dark said. "It has been known by different names, by the Greeks, the Egyptians, the Romans, but it was brought together in the sixteenth century by its then leader—da Vinci. The Council as we know it today, that set up the Academies to guide those with gifts such as the two of you, started as a body of people who safeguarded the wisdom of the world."

"Huh?" Xavier said.

Sam almost took pleasure in knowing more than Xavier about something for once—almost. But this was not the time to gloat.

"They've been entrusted with preserving what we know," Dr. Dark said, "secretly making sure that humanity keeps moving forward, even in the so-called Dark Ages, when the Council were forced underground, persecuted and hunted down for what they knew."

"But how come—I mean . . ." Xavier looked at Sam and then back to his father, as though it made sense to them yet he was just hearing it for the first time. "Why have I, or the world, not heard about them before?"

"Dreamers are everywhere—teachers at schools and universities, our leaders, our family, our friends. Or just people you see on the bus. Dreamers, including those on the Council, are around us every day. And those who form the Council of Dreamers have been meeting in Paris for over two hundred years, protecting our heritage until the moment came when Dreamers would be revealed to the world."

"Are you saying that *you're* on the Council?" Xavier asked slowly.

"Yes, son," Dr. Dark said. "And hopefully one day, you will be too."

"*Me?*" Xavier said in surprise. Xavier turned from his dad to Sam. "Is this all making sense to you? A secret group who meets to make sure we—what, we safeguard wisdom?"

"Yeah." Sam looked at his friend. "I've heard bits and pieces already, seen some stuff, so I'm pretty convinced. It's true, Xav."

"Why are we Dreamers?" Xavier asked his dad.

"We are the lucky ones, blessed with a gift. We understand that the human mind is capable of so much more, via our subconscious mind in our dreams, and so much more good is possible for humanity."

"So why are people trying to kill us?" Xavier asked.

Dr. Dark let out a long breath.

"Where there is good, there is the other. There are those who want the knowledge we safeguard for their own gain—and their intentions for such power would spell disaster."

"But why us? Why *Sam*?" Xavier persisted.

"Sam is one of the last 13."

"The what?" Xavier asked, then looked to Sam.

"He's a special Dreamer," Dr. Dark said, "one of thirteen who will make a stand against evil."

"What?" Xavier laughed nervously as Sam shook his head and shrugged, as though saying, *all in a day.*

"The mind is a powerful thing," Dr. Dark said. "Sam was created with the aid of modern scientific genius," Dr. Dark chuckled to himself over that, "to help us find the very thing that formed the Council in the first place."

"And that is . . ."

"The greatest treasure of ancient knowledge and power ever accumulated."

The car slowed as the driver took an exit ramp, and they were soon weaving their way along gravelled lanes and then through heavily forested grounds, the whole time Xavier and his father trading back and forth the details of the Dreamer world that Sam was becoming ever more familiar with.

"Ah," Dr. Dark said, pointing at what looked like a palatial stately home. "We're here."

14

EVA

After a restless sleep, Eva got up, showered and put on her Academy uniform. She stood next to the window, cradling a cup of tea in her cold hands. Outside, in the gloom of the overcast afternoon full of dark snow clouds, the little pinprick of light flickered on a neighbouring mountain. Eva stared out into the distance for a long time.

"What is it?" Gabriella asked, coming up behind her.

"It's a camp fire," Eva said.

"Who could be out there?" Gabriella asked.

Eva shook her head. "Lora sent out some Guardians to check it out before but they couldn't find anyone."

Eva remained staring out the window as the view fogged over with dark cloud. Gabriella went into the small adjoining bathroom, and Eva heard the shower hissing moments later.

"So you did not know that your parents weren't your real parents?" Gabriella asked as she emerged from the bathroom a long time later. She was dressed in an Academy uniform, a towel still wrapped around her wet hair. Gabriella pulled at the fabric as she looked at herself in the mirror. She sighed.

"No," Eva said, sitting on her bed, leaning back.

"And they were . . . these Enterprise people?" Gabriella said.

"Agents. Yep."

"And my parents?" Gabriella replied. "I should call my father but I have no phone."

"I don't know. Ask the Professor, he might know more, maybe you can call him," Eva said, checking her watch. She sighed deeply. "But the last 13 could be anyone."

"And they have dreams like my dream about the disc in the Pantheon?" Gabriella asked.

"Yeah, I think so." Eva looked at Gabriella. Even standing there in the same boring uniform as Eva, Gabriella still seemed to radiate an air of glamour and excitement. She had fitted into this new and unfamiliar world so immediately, a social chameleon adapting with ease.

"Knock, knock," Lora interrupted, her head appearing around the door. "You two OK?"

"Fine," Eva and Gabriella said at the same time.

"Good. Still no word from Sam, but we know he's alright, he's outside Berlin now," Lora said, motioning for the girls to follow her. "And if you'll come with me, there's something you can help us with."

"Welcome back, Eva," the Professor said kindly, giving her shoulder a light squeeze. "And Gabriella, we meet at last. I'm a big fan."

Gabriella flashed her immense smile and shook his hand.

"So glad you're here. The accommodation is sufferable, I hope?" the Professor added with a wry grin

Gabriella's cheeks flushed a little and she nodded. It was the first time Eva had seen Gabriella looking somewhat self-conscious.

Eva had expected to be meeting the Professor in his office, to go over all that had happened in Rome. Instead, they were in a room Eva had not seen before. A large table encircled by chairs filled the centre space and two large screens hung on the walls. Eva could see a video camera set up in the corner.

The Professor indicated that they should sit at the table just as Lora and Jedi entered the room.

"Now, Lora has given me a full run-down of everything that occurred in Rome," the Professor began. "We have managed to pinpoint where Sam is in Germany, and Jedi is currently looking into the best and safest way to make contact," the Professor continued. "He obviously wanted to fly solo for a while but I'm sure he'll want to be in touch soon. When this happens, we will of course invite you to take part in the conversation. Now, Gabriella," the Professor looked at her directly, his tone serious. "There are a concerning number of theories circulating, growing by the minute, about your involvement in the incident in Rome and your whereabouts now. We feel we need to deal with this immediately and directly. You do understand why you need to stay here? I have no doubt that your role in the race as one of the last 13 will continue yet. You will not be safe in Rome."

"*Si*. Yes, I understand," Gabriella nodded again.

"Lora and Jedi have organized for you to film a message for the media, so everyone knows you're OK. If you agree, we think it best if you also announce that you will be taking a well-needed break from the music scene."

Gabriella thought for a long moment. "Yes, yes . . . I could say that what happened in Roma has affected me deeply . . . I am now too worried for my safety, and I need much time to think," she said. Then she added, "Perhaps I tell them I will be using my time away to work on my skills as an actress? I have always wanted to be in the movies."

Eva scoffed before she could stop herself. She imagined Gabriella's over-the-top, teary farewell to the world's waiting media.

She's a pretty good actress already.

Eva caught Lora's inquisitive look but pretended not to see it.

"Wonderful suggestion," the Professor agreed. "Lora will help you with the broadcast and whatever preparations you need. And of course you will want to call your family, we can arrange that also." Gabriella beamed.

"Now, Eva," the Professor shifted his gaze to her, "we know you are deeply concerned about Sam, and keen to help in whatever way you can—"

"Yes, absolutely!" Eva cut in, eagerly. "I can have my stuff ready in five minutes and go wherever you need me to go."

"Well, that won't be too far, as it happens," the Professor said. "Jedi needs your help in his office, investigating the pages in the journal and the gear piece that Gabriella and Sam located in Rome. Time is of the essence and we believe there is important information in that book that could help Sam."

"Oh, OK," Eva said quietly, trying to hide her disappointment from everyone, especially Jedi. She looked over and gave him a quick smile. "Whatever's most helpful to Sam."

15

SAM

The black Mercedes roared its way along a birch-lined gravel driveway that led them through acres of lush pastures. Xavier had told his father of his concerns for Ahmed, and despite several phone calls trying to discover his whereabouts which led to no further answers, Dr. Dark did not look too worried.

"I've known Ahmed a long time, and he can be somewhat . . . unpredictable, so I shouldn't worry too much," he said.

"But he said he was trying to get a message to Sam and I swear I heard him say 'they're coming' just before the line dropped out," Xavier argued.

"It could have been a taxi coming, or any number of other possibilities. You know your godfather, he loves to go adventuring in far-flung places, I suspect he's just off on an archaeological adventure now," Dr. Dark waved his hand at Xavier's imminent protest. "I'm sure he'll be back in touch soon."

Xavier fell silent as the road wound its way through manicured gardens.

"Where are we?" Sam asked.

"This house belongs to an associate of mine," Dr. Dark said.

"This associate a king or something?" Sam asked. "This is some house."

Sam craned his neck to see the full height of the building as they approached. It was long and square, made from sandstone, three stories tall, with a sloped slate roof and a tower at either end. "Do all you rich people just hang out together all the time?"

Dr. Dark smiled. "He's from a long line of noble men who have helped our cause."

"*Hans* helps out Dreamers?" Xavier said.

"Yes."

"Well, I still don't like him. There's something off about that guy," Xavier said.

"You'll be polite while we are guests in his home," Dr. Dark told his son, who rolled his eyes in reply.

"Fine," Xavier said, then turned to Sam and whispered. "I've met him a few times, you'll see."

"Well, whoever this Hans guy is, he sure is rich," Sam said as they passed a carved stone fountain the size of the grandest ones he'd seen in Italy.

"Sam, you'll find that those of us who true dream seem to do quite well, *if* we choose to," Dr. Dark replied as they pulled up to the entry portico.

"Because you can see into the future?" Xavier asked.

"Yes—but we don't use it for pure economic gain, like playing the stock market or gambling," Dr. Dark replied. "The Council looks very sternly upon that sort of thing."

"Does Hans know about what's happening at the moment? With the prophecy and everything?" Sam said.

"No," he replied. "But he knows of my work with true dreams, and he's been a very generous backer over the years, helping to fund the Council and the Academy."

A butler came out and Dr. Dark greeted him warmly, "Otto! Good to see you again, and so good of you to have us here at such short notice."

"So, why don't you like Hans?" Sam asked Xavier quietly as they got out of the car.

"He's just . . ." Xavier whispered, "weird. Always acts like he's better than everyone, talks over people. Laughs funny too, like a hyena. And his breath smells like bad cheese— you'd think he'd just thrown up in his own mouth."

"That's a lovely image, thanks," Sam whispered back. "It's making me think of our security guard buddy back in Cairo." Sam pulled a face and Xavier snorted with laughter.

The butler turned to them abruptly and gave them a stony stare. He motioned them inside the house with a stiff wave of his gloved hand.

"Our host is not here at the moment, but we can stay as long as we need to," Dr. Dark said. They went inside, following the butler into a grand library with plush leather chairs. A songbird swinging in a gilt cage next to the fireplace let out an elegant trill as Sam came closer for a look.

"We'll be safe here for a while," Dr. Dark said as he sat down and made himself comfortable. "Until I talk to the Professor and the Council and see what the current situation is, it's best we stay hidden."

Otto came back in with a tray piled high with drinks and food.

"So, why *were* you two at the museum archives?" Dr. Dark asked finally.

"To find clues," Sam said.

"Xavier?" Dr. Dark questioned.

"He's telling the truth, Dad," Xavier said. "We went to see what was there, what Ahmed had left behind."

"And this rubbing of the Stele was about the only thing there, apart from reams of field notes and recordings," Sam added, pulling the paper out of his backpack.

"How did you know about it being stored there?" Dr. Dark asked.

"Sam dreamed it," Xavier blurted out. He gave Sam a meaningful look.

"Sam? Is this true?"

Sam nodded. *Why doesn't he want his father to know he was the one who dreamed of it?*

Dr. Dark stood up and went to the bar where he poured himself another coffee. "Show me," he said.

Sam unrolled the tracing paper.

"Incredible . . ." Dr. Dark said, taking in the sight of the rubbing laid out in full on a large table in the centre of the library. "For centuries people searched for this missing half of the Stele in Egypt and all along it was lying forgotten in Cyprus—and then suddenly it was gone. How marvellous we had a copy of it sitting in our archives."

"What's the big deal?" Xavier asked.

"It holds the second half of the prophecy," Sam said. "The one about the last 13." He walked around the rubbing, taking photos with his phone. With the touch of a button, he emailed them to Jedi. *Won't they just lose their minds at the Academy when they see this?*

"This Dream Stele is more than a representation of a moment of Ramses' time," Dr. Dark was saying. "It's part of something bigger."

"Part of . . ." Sam began.

Dr. Dark looked up. ". . . the fate of the world."

16

ALEX

"**A**bsolutely not," Stella said, not skipping a beat in her fast-paced stride as she walked into the hangar, the clicking of her shoes echoing loudly.

"But Jack said that I—"

Stella stopped abruptly and gave Alex a look that could kill. She came close to his face. "I have worked with some of the world's top military teams," she said. "I've seen more combat and been shot at more times than you could ever dream of. I'm not about to jeopardize the success of my mission so a jumped-up teenager can tag along."

With that, she turned on her heel and walked away.

Alex watched her toss her pack to the loadmaster and she climbed the stairs into the Enterprise's jet, a compact airliner. About a dozen Agents had boarded, all of them in their trademark grey suits, white shirts and black ties. One guy was loading bags through the cargo doors underneath the windows while other logistics guys carted equipment to him. Alex pulled his backpack on and edged nearer. He noticed that there was quite a lot of room inside the cargo hold . . . *enough space for a jumped-up teenager*. He grinned. Alex made a bed out of soft duffel bags and braced himself for take off. The bumpy taxiing bounced him around, his gut churning as he heard the engines powering up. His hands over his ears, he nearly let out a whoop of excitement when the aircraft left the tarmac and banked into the sky. Once the landing gear had been raised, it was surprisingly quiet in the cargo hold.

He rummaged through a couple of bags and found a small flashlight and some magazines to read. Half an hour in and he'd turned every page of them and not taken in a word.

Seeing as I'm going to be in here for a while, I may as well get my beauty sleep.

Alex got comfortable and closed his eyes.

He woke with a start and checked the time on his phone. A few hours had slipped by. He smiled at the thought of being asked to switch off electronic devices and phones by an air steward—*not down here!* Then he hurriedly switched his phone to airplane mode, just in case.

Now he needed to dream up some brilliant scheme to give Stella the slip so he could secretly follow her team into the field . . .

Dreaming . . .

A dream! I'll tell her that I was holding something back before—that I'd had a dream about being there, in Berlin with her, and that we found Sam together! Then she'll have to take me along.

His stomach growled and Alex was instantly reminded that he'd forgotten to pack any food when he'd "borrowed" supplies from the Enterprise storerooms. He rummaged through the closest bags and got lucky with some sports drinks and snacks. He ate a chocolate bar and scrolled to his favourite band on his phone while he pictured how he could stay one step ahead of Stella.

Alex knew they were coming in to land when he heard the flaps engage for descent, and soon the landing gear came down. He pocketed his phone and braced for the landing as well as he could, tucked in-between a stack of suitcases and bags.

With no visual clues to gauge their approach, the landing was a sudden and abrupt impact, followed by the deafening sound of the reverse thrusters of the engines.

Alex swore and then clamped his hands over his mouth, panicking that he could have been loud enough to be heard through the floor of the passenger compartment above. He calmed his breathing and heart rate, and then sent a text message through to Phoebe just so that she knew what he'd done . . . *and in case Stella actually kills me for turning up unannounced.*

Within a few minutes he felt the aircraft come to a stop, and heard the built-in stairs fold out. Another minute and the cargo doors were opened. The two Agents unloading the bags and cases were quick and efficient, putting the bags into the rear of a couple of vans parked in a private hangar.

Alex slid out when they both had their backs to him, and he walked up to Stella, who was on the phone. When she hung up the call and turned to face him she didn't seem surprised.

"So," she said, looking at him through squinting eyes. "I'm told you had a dream that you had to be here."

"Yes, I was going to—"

She held up her hand for him to stop and he didn't need to be told twice.

"Get in, we'll talk later."

She walked away, and Alex headed for the closest van, but it was already full of unfriendly Agents, all looking at him like he was an unwelcome dead weight. He found a small space, albeit equally hostile, in the other van. They rolled out of the airport and headed toward Berlin city in the darkness of the night.

After a short ride, they pulled up to a small business hotel and Alex found Stella in the lobby.

"What are we doing here?" Alex asked her.

She looked at him.

"Shouldn't we be out there," Alex said, "looking for Sam?"

She pointed to the doors of the hotel that led back out to the street. "Be my guest," Stella said. "Berlin's a big city though, and you wouldn't have to be one of the last 13 to attract attention out there all alone in the middle of the night."

Alex's gaze fell from the dark empty street outside to the carpeted floor at his feet.

"I thought so," Stella said, then barked orders to the Agents who split up to go to their rooms. Alex caught her at the elevators.

"Wait," he said, "are we here to work, or just to sleep?"

The elevator pinged its arrival.

"I'm here to work, and I'll do that as I best know how." Stella walked into the elevator. She turned and looked at him, and before the doors closed, she put out her arm to delay it. Her eyes were steel-blue and unflinching. "*Did* you have a dream that was relevant to my mission?"

Alex was cornered in that stare.

"Yes," he lied. He knew he hadn't fooled her but she simply nodded and stepped back into the elevator. "Wait— what do I do?" he called.

"Your roommate's behind you," Stella said as the elevator doors closed.

Slowly, Alex turned around.

A mountain of a man stood there, looking at him. His head was as large as a kitchen pot, his ape-like arms hanging down his sides, his knuckles nearly at his knees. *This guy's bigger than the drinks machine at school.*

"Hey," Alex said by way of greeting.

The Agent grunted a reply, hefted his bag over his shoulder, and pressed the elevator call button.

"My name's Alex," Alex said, offering his hand but it was left dangling. Alex swallowed hard.

"I know who you are," the guy replied, getting into the elevator. "You drank my sports drinks."

17

SAM

"**S**o," Dr. Dark said. "Why don't we settle in and the two of you can tell me about your most recent dreams?"

Xavier seemed to have finally given up all hope of hiding anything from his father, so Sam and he recounted their dreams, demolishing a plate of cakes in the process. Sam sat on the floor, stretching out, while Xavier sat opposite his dad by the fire and looked nervous, as if he might be laughed at or told off.

"Hmm, so there's no doubt . . ." Dr. Dark said, staring up at the ceiling as he sipped his whiskey.

Sam felt as though he were back in the doctor's suite in Vancouver and thought of all those years they'd discussed his dreams. His Agent parents had sent him there.

Eva too . . .

"Wait—tell me . . . what's the connection between you, the Professor, and the Enterprise guy—their boss? Do you know each other? How come you ended up treating Enterprise-created kids? Did they put you up to it?"

"Well, let me start at the beginning." Dr. Dark sat upright

in his chair and put his drink down. "I studied at the Sorbonne with Tom—the Professor—and Jack, but soon after our studies we went our separate ways to pursue our post-doctoral work."

"What?" Sam said. "Hold on a minute. So all *three* of you knew each other at university?"

"That's where we met, in Paris, in a class given by a very learned Dreamer who has, sadly, since passed away," Dr. Dark said. "Tom was convinced that all dreaming abilities could be taught—true dreams, applying dreams in the waking world, all of it."

Dr. Dark sat forward in his chair as he continued.

"Jack and I—we both thought this extra dreaming ability had more to do with our *genes*—and that those of us with the right genetic makeup were able to tap into it."

"Nature versus nurture, right?" Sam said.

"Yes, that's how our differences of opinion started, although Jack and I soon disagreed on *how* we thought the innate talent should be fostered—and to what extent it could be."

"Disagreed how?" Sam said. "Because he wanted to control what we would become in a lab?"

"That's oversimplifying it," Dr. Dark said, "but yes, you could say that."

"And you?" Xavier said.

"I wanted to give Mother Nature a helping hand by enhancing what was innately in you, in all of us, already—I thought we could find the middle ground between nature and nurture through cognitive science." Dr. Dark poured himself a glass of water. "But Jack mapped a gene variation that helped people live into their nineties and beyond. It also aided memory and learning in the elderly. It altered the size of cholesterol particles, making them less likely to cause strokes. People aged ninety-five or older who had the gene variant were twice as likely to have good brain function. From there he worked with researchers to discover more about how they could manipulate brain function through genetics."

"What's the connection to true dreams?" Sam said.

Dark smiled. "They call it the Dreamer Gene."

18

EVA

"Should we wait for your new friend, the pop star?" Jedi teased.

"She's not my friend, she's a roommate who's been forced upon me," Eva complained.

"Aw, come on, she can't be that bad? Where is she, anyway?"

"Signing more autographs, probably." Eva pulled a face and Jedi raised his eyebrows at her. "OK, I think she's still with Lora recording her 'broadcast to her fans,' and talking to her family. And then I guess she's got a bit of last 13 history to catch up on. So it's just us for now, and I like it like that," she finally smiled once more and Jedi looked happy.

They were back in Jedi's lab, the sound of computers humming all around them as he brought them some drinks.

"So, how can I be of service?" Eva smiled.

"I have something rather special to show you," Jedi proclaimed. "Come take a look at this and feast your eyes on history."

"O . . . kay . . ." Eva followed him to a high white table in the corner of the room. She pulled up a stool alongside him and turned her attention to the book he placed in front of her.

"This is the book Sam and Gabriella found in Rome, isn't it?" she asked.

"Sure is . . . take a closer look," Jedi urged.

Eva examined the ancient book carefully. She fumbled to turn the pages, the cotton gloves Jedi made her put on hindering her progress. They were full of diagrams and notations in almost-illegible writing.

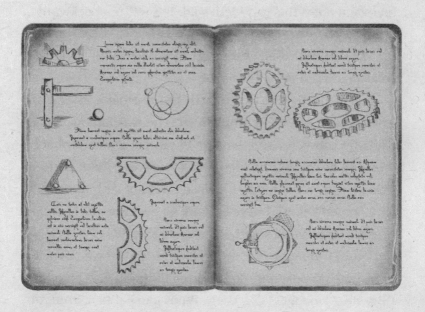

Her drink sat untouched on Jedi's desk as she became more and more absorbed in the pages. *There's something special about this book . . .*

"What *is* it?" she asked, looking up at him eagerly. "Do you know?"

"I did some reading up earlier and the Professor and I believe it's part of a sixteenth century journal," Jedi said, taking it from her in his own gloved hands.

"What language is it written in?"

"Italian," Jedi replied.

"That doesn't look like Italian," Eva said. "Are you sure?"

"That's because Leonardo da Vinci wrote most of his personal notes this way," Jedi said. "It's written backwards, right to left."

"*This* journal was written by da Vinci?" *Wow, he wasn't kidding about it being "history."*

Jedi nodded. "He wrote both the normal way and in this kind of 'mirror writing.' In fact, he was famous for it. Nobody knows for sure why he did it, but it was probably because he was left-handed and it was easier." Jedi noticed Eva's frown and added, "He wasn't writing with a modern pen, remember, he'd have had ink all over the place, and it was easier to avoid smudging the other way."

"Huh, I thought you were going to say it was to write down secrets or something exciting like that," Eva laughed. "But no—smudges. OK, then. What journal is it from, do you know?"

"You bet I know. It's one of the most famous collections of writing in the world—the *Codex Atlanticus*," he said with a flourish.

"Hold on, I think I've heard of that," Eva said. She could see the wonder on Jedi's face, but she couldn't recall enough about the Codex to share in his amazement just yet.

"Written and illustrated by da Vinci—his greatest collection of work," Jedi prompted. "I can't believe they found it in Rome. In the Vatican library of all places!"

"I'm sorry, you're going to have to remind me," Eva said with a sheepish grin. "What's the *Codex Atlanticus*?"

"The *Codex Atlanticus* is made up of twelve volumes of drawings and writings, all by da Vinci. It's over a thousand pages of his notes on mathematics, musical instruments, war machines, powered flight, botany . . . anything and everything he was interested in. The original is in a library in Milan."

"And *this* is part of it?" Eva asked.

"I think we're looking at the missing thirteenth volume," Jedi said. "*Navigation and time instruments.* Look here," Jedi said. "This diagram . . ."

They studied the page. It showed a diagram of a machine, the shape and size of a shoebox, with measurements and notations among the meticulous detail.

"It can't be a coincidence," Eva whispered, taking the book back from Jedi to look even closer.

"What?" Jedi peered over her shoulder, passing her a magnifying glass.

"Check out this part here," she said, holding the glass over the enlarged diagram of the side view.

"A star-shaped hole." Jedi looked at Eva. "I guess we know where that key goes, then?"

"When was this volume lost?" Eva asked.

"It says here the Codex was taken from Milan by the French during the Napoleonic occupation," Jedi said, bringing up research from the Internet, "and only partly returned after 1815."

"Are you thinking what I'm thinking?" Eva said.

Jedi nodded. "Yup. If you're thinking that the last 13 have to—"

An insistent and high-pitched beeping across the room grabbed their attention. Jedi slid over in his chair to take a closer look.

"What's up? Everything OK?" Eva asked, coming over to join him. Several screens flashed and bleeped frantically.

"These are alerts—they go off whenever specific trigger words or phrases come up on the Internet." He flicked between several screens, scanning quicker than Eva could read. "I set up searches to monitor particular sites, you know, international police sites, conspiracy blogs, that kind of thing. And it looks like our race isn't going to be a secret for much longer."

WWW.THECLANDESTINECLOAK.COM

HOME

LATEST NEWS

TRUTH VAULT

ABOUT

CONTACT

SEARCH SITE

WHO DO YOU BELIEVE?

Our governments would have you believe that the recent spate of violent events around the world are just a coicindance, but here at The Clandestine Cloak, we know there is a much larger conspiracy at work.

The attacks in Egypt that were meant to be the work of treasure hunters? The destruction of the Dream Stele in the New York Museum of Natural History? These were not just random events, these were the work of a secret society, determined to conceal an ancient treasure that should rightly belong to the whole world.

But just who are the people in this society of the shadows? Click here for Daniel Lowcombe's exposé on the black market in Ancient Egyptian relics.

Join the conversation at
www.theclandestinecloak.com/membersforum

19

SAM

"And of course, da Vinci is at the heart of it all," Dr. Dark had a captive audience now—Sam and Xavier were rooted to the spot.

"Da Vinci?" Sam said. "I should have known."

"He was an astonishing artist and inventor, a genius in many ways," Dr. Dark said. "But he was something even more special. He was one of the most powerful Dreamers who's ever lived. And that was Jack's final leap, his greatest step forward, and it's why you're special too."

"What's this got to do with da Vinci?" Sam asked.

"You've seen *Jurassic Park*, correct?" Dr. Dark said. "I know Xavier has, many times."

"Totally, yeah," Xavier said.

"Seen it and read it," Sam replied.

"Good. So, you know that in the story they created dinosaurs using DNA sequencing? Well, Jack and his team of lab coats at the Enterprise managed to map the DNA of da Vinci, and found a certain uncommon gene, which he then applied to you."

"What?" Sam stood and paced the room. "So I'm— I'm what? I'm *related* to da Vinci?"

"Not really. One of your genes is cloned from his," Dr. Dark said, "but it's really a tiny part of your genetic makeup. That was always Jack's plan, even at university," Dr. Dark said. "To create a blueprint for genetic genius. So people would be able to dream beyond what anyone else could achieve."

"And what about now? I'm fifteen. Whatever Jack did to my DNA, that was a long time ago," Sam said.

"That's right. Imagine what the Enterprise scientists could have achieved by now," Dr. Dark said, staring into the fire. "Just imagine . . ."

"*Could* have achieved?" Sam asked.

"You were the last, Sam. The program was shut down by the United States government," Dr. Dark explained. "Where do you think their funding was coming from?" he added.

Sam didn't know what to make of it all, and by the look on Xavier's face, he didn't either. Yet, he had to admit it was making sense.

But how does that help me now?

"So that's why we were made? To give someone, some government an advantage?" Sam said. "Shame they couldn't have made me without asthma."

Both Xavier and his father chuckled.

"It's not so much that you were both 'made,'" Dr. Dark said. "It's more that—"

"Wait," Xavier said, interrupting his father. "You said 'both.' Do you mean . . . Dad?"

Dr. Dark swallowed hard.

"Dad—am I . . . ?" Xavier stood. "Are you even my real—?"

"Calm down," Dr. Dark said. "I am your father, don't ever think otherwise."

"But did you—I mean, am I some kind of *experiment?*"

Dr. Dark took a moment to answer, settling himself to share a piece of information he'd waited a lifetime to pass on.

"Yes, Xavier," he said, "you have the same enhanced DNA as Sam. But I am your father, and your mother was your mother. Don't get carried away."

Xavier walked around the room, trying to take this news in.

"Son, it's a *gift*—" Dr. Dark began.

"I'm a freak!" Xavier shouted. He glared at his father as he raged. "A mutant!"

"No, son, you're *special*, you truly have a gift, you just have to apply it," Dr. Dark said, in his well-practised soothing doctor voice. "If humanity decides that we need to do more to exploit human talent, then we will all benefit. You possess genetic assets beyond the ordinary, while so many out there are suffering from an inability, so far, to tap into what they already have."

"Why didn't you tell me about any of this sooner?" Xavier asked. "Why do I find out now, like this?"

Sam sat back in his chair, uncomfortable to be in the presence of the family revelations rocking the room.

"Dad—why didn't you tell me before?"

"You weren't ready," Dr. Dark sighed.

"When would I be?" Xavier shot back.

"Now."

"Why?" Xavier asked. "Why now?"

Dr. Dark turned his attention to Sam. "Sam, am I right in assuming that Xavier is not here by accident?"

Sam felt his face redden as he slowly nodded and looked anxiously at Xavier.

"And would I also be right in assuming that he's part of the race?" he continued.

Sam nodded again.

Dr. Dark stood and went to his son and put a hand on his shoulder and looked him in the eye. "Xavier, I've been waiting for the right time, and that time is now. You and Sam are part of something that will shape the world in ways that we cannot even imagine yet. I believe *you* are also one of the last 13."

20

Sam grabbed his bag and left the room to give Xavier and his dad privacy to talk. He was guiltily grateful that Dr. Dark would be the one to explain the last 13 to Xavier and all that was going to mean for him.

I can't believe Dr. Dark is a Dreamer, on the Council of Dreamers! The whole time he was my doctor he knew all about this other world, and then it turns out his patient is one of the last 13. And his son!

Sam couldn't quite work out if he should be angry with Dr. Dark for hiding the Dreaming world from him. Then he remembered Tobias and his "parents" had all known, or suspected, that he might become a Dreamer. *And* possibly one of the last 13. His head hurt thinking about it and he decided to just let it go for now.

He wandered through the expanse of the massive house in search of food. In the huge kitchen, Sam fixed himself a sandwich from the fridge.

"So, let's look at what we have here . . ." Sam took out the rubbing of the Dream Stele from where he'd slotted it back into his pack and laid it out on the slab of white marble of the island bench. It certainly *looked* like an exact fit to the top half of the Stele. Looking at it, he couldn't imagine what, if anything, it was revealing.

Why go to all the trouble of destroying every trace of it? Perhaps there's a detail here, a clue to what the prophecy will reveal. Sam studied it closely. Try as he might, there was nothing he could learn from it without Jedi's translation.

"Sam, there you are," Dr. Dark said, coming into the room. "The Professor is on the phone, he'd like to speak to you."

Sam spoke to the Professor at length, while Xavier and his father watched and waited. Xavier's eyes looked red and Dr. Dark took the time to compose himself after what had obviously been a heated argument.

Sam focused on discussing what had happened since the events in Rome. The Academy staff were already busy trying to decipher digital images of the rubbing he'd sent to Jedi— the place was abuzz with the news that the inscription on the missing half of the Stele had been found after all.

Sam then said hello to Eva, Lora and Gabriella as they joined the conversation. The three of them were in high spirits to hear from him. Finally Jedi came on the line and Sam put Dr. Dark's phone on speaker so they could all share in the conversation.

"Sam, good to hear that you're in one piece," Jedi said. "Much better than two pieces. Or three, for that matter."

"Thanks, Jedi," Sam said. "Right back at you."

"Now, that Gear you found in the pulpit of the church in Rome?"

"Gear?" Sam said.

"The brass disc with teeth all around—it's a Gear," Jedi replied. "Part of a machine."

"Egyptian?" Sam asked.

"No, I don't think so," Jedi said. "Eva and I have been examining the journal that Gabriella found in the Vatican library and we believe it holds the answer."

"Go on," Sam urged, noticing Dr. Dark leaning forward and listening intently.

"The journal was da Vinci's, and in it there are several drawings and notes about a machine," Jedi said. Sam listened, stunned at the news. *More da Vinci?*

"It's a bit of a leap of faith at this point, but I think the machine he refers to as the 'Bakhu' is what will show us the way in this race."

"Bakhu?" Sam asked.

"It comes from an Egyptian myth," Jedi replied. "It was the name of the mountain from which the sun rose."

"Well, I guess it's not surprising that da Vinci would have made an Egyptian connection," Sam said.

"Exactly," Eva said. "And we think the Bakhu is the very thing the last 13 are racing to find."

EVA

"It's true, Sam," Eva said, the phone on the table between her, Gabriella, Jedi, Lora and the Professor. "This is what the last 13 are destined to do. To build the machine."

"Like putting together a puzzle, do you mean?" Xavier said over the phone.

"Sort of—there's a section in the journal that talks about the thirteen pieces that complete the Bakhu. We're still translating right now but it seems like this is really it. Da Vinci even mentions specially made Gears."

"Like the Gear we found in Italy, Sam? It must be a part that goes inside the machine, yes?" Gabriella said.

"And Sam?" Eva continued.

"Yep, I'm here," he replied.

"There's a star-shaped hole on the outside of the machine."

"Whoa."

"Well said, Sam," the Professor chimed in. "I think we're truly now beginning to see our purpose in this race."

"It all makes sense, doesn't it?" Sam replied. "The Star of Egypt was da Vinci's and the key was inside. Then the Gear in Rome . . . so what does the machine do?" Sam asked. "Do the Gears make it a clock or something?"

"If I may address that question," Dr. Dark said. "As most of you now know, there have long been rumours in the Dreamer world of the prophecy leading to some kind of ultimate power," Dr. Dark said. "The prophecies that the Council have studied and safeguarded all these years point to writings through the ages, from Egyptian and Greek and Roman times, right through to the Renaissance, of a gateway to a world of impossible treasures. Just what the—"

Jedi cut in, "Excuse me, Doc. I think we can help you out there. My Renaissance Italian might be a bit rusty but we're pretty sure we've found numerous mentions in the journal to something called 'the Dream Gate.'"

"I knew it!" Dr. Dark exclaimed.

"Don't let's get ahead of ourselves, Dark," the Professor cautioned.

"Dream Gate?" Sam said. "A gate *into* the dream world? To tap into more of our minds?"

"I see you've got to him, Professor," Dr. Dark said. "Well, that is one possibility, Sam, one *interpretation*."

"And it is as good as any," the Professor replied.

"Perhaps," Dr. Dark said. "But what's important at the moment is finding the last 13 in order to build this machine. Correct, Professor?"

"Yes," the Professor replied, his voice wary. "It is important, there's no denying that."

Eva looked at the Professor. He suddenly looked much older. *Everyone looks so serious now, even Gabriella.*

"So there are thirteen pieces, scattered around the world, hidden even, or perhaps in plain sight, such as the piece in Rome," Eva said.

"Who put them there?" Lora asked.

"Well, that we may never fully know," the Professor said, "especially if they have moved more recently. But we know who made them, who invented this machine, and what its purpose is."

"So we put the Bakhu together, with all these Gears and the key," Eva said, joining the dots, "and it will show us where the Dream Gate is."

"And whatever lies beyond," the Professor concluded.

"Exactly," Dr. Dark replied, and Eva saw the Professor and Jedi nodding.

"Get the Gears, build the machine. Build the machine, find the Gate," Eva said.

"Find the Gate," Sam said, "save the world."

SAM

Sam and Xavier sat at one end of an enormous dining table with Dr. Dark seated next to them, reading over some notes. Dinner was soon brought out on silver trays and served table-side by the butler.

"Ah, if only you two were old enough to appreciate this fine wine," Dr. Dark said, sipping his glass of merlot. Xavier and Sam raised their juices in a mock salute.

Sam waited until Otto left, and then said, "So this machine with the thirteen pieces—does it mean that da Vinci knew about the prophecy?"

"Yes, that's the only logical explanation," Dr. Dark said. "Unless . . . well, what exactly he knew about the last 13 is unclear, but we always knew he had collected information about the prophecy."

"So we have a key and a Gear," Sam said. "Now we have to find the other Dreamers—in order to find the other pieces through their dreams."

"Precisely."

"It was Gabriella who led me to the Rome Gear," Sam

said. "So, where's the piece that Xavier leads us to?"

Xavier's face creased in disappointment.

"At the right time," Dr. Dark said, looking to his son, "the dream will come again and you'll remember. You can't force these things."

"You said to the Professor that tapping into the mind," Sam said, "entering into the dream world, was just one interpretation of the ultimate goal?"

"Yes," Dr. Dark said, his eyebrows raised. "Good to see you were listening."

"But it's not *your* interpretation?" Sam asked.

"Well . . . yes and no," Dr. Dark replied. "It goes deeper than that."

"What is it?" Xavier added.

"The prophecy and all related writings say it will lead to a treasure so great that it will eclipse all others."

"Treasure?" Sam said.

"Beyond what you can imagine," Dr. Dark said.

"Dessert, sirs," Otto said, magically appearing back at the table and placing an apple strudel and a selection of ice cream in front of them.

"Thank you," Dr. Dark said, "but I don't think we could fit in another thing."

"I could," Sam said. "Easily."

"Me too," Xavier said, patting his bulging belly. "I'm not scared of a little post-dinner gas."

The two of them cracked up laughing.

"Very well, leave it here, thank you," Dr. Dark said to the butler. "We won't be needing anything else this evening. Good night, Otto."

"And a good night to you and the young sirs," he replied, closing the door as he left.

"I so need a butler one day," Sam said, digging into a slice of strudel with ice cream. "How good is this?"

"I know, right?" Xavier said through a mouthful. His dad just shook his head and chuckled.

"So what's next for us?" Sam asked.

"We get you back to the Academy in the morning," Dr. Dark said. "It's the safest place for you to be until we know where to go next."

"So we stay here for the night?" Xavier asked. "This place is cool, but it's a bit creepy if you ask me."

"It's safer this way," Dr. Dark replied.

As Sam began to feel too full to move, he was grateful for this little reprieve. He looked at Xavier and wondered if they'd find out where to go next that very night.

"Well, let's call it an evening," Dr. Dark said, standing up from the table, yawning. "It's been one hell of a day for everyone."

"You're sure we're safe here?" Sam said as he followed Xavier and his dad from the room and up the stairs.

"Of course," Dr. Dark replied. "Only the Academy know

we're here."

"You'll forgive me if I don't feel too safe *anywhere* at the moment," Sam said. "What with my recent brushes with the German Guardians and all."

They were silent as they walked down a long carpeted corridor.

"Is this our room?" Xavier asked as they stopped by the open door a few paces farther down the hall. There were two luxurious single beds, the blankets turned down and the reading lamps on.

"Yes, Otto prepared your room earlier, and I'm just across the hall if you need me," Dr. Dark said. "Good night, boys. Try to sleep well."

Sam and Xavier settled into their beds in the guest wing of the house. Sam turned off his lamp and turned to face Xavier. He was perched on his own bed, reading about something on his tablet.

"Hey, Sam, tell me about your dream, the one you had before we came to Berlin," Xavier said.

"My dream?" Sam said. "Well, it was more a series of snapshots, a bunch of little scenes."

Xavier was quiet for a while, and Sam noticed him put down his computer.

"So, how does it work?" Xavier asked. "When you have

these dreams, or premonitions or whatever . . . ?"

"I honestly don't know," Sam shrugged.

"Do you know when you're going to dream like that?"

"No, it's exactly like any other dream—only it comes true very soon after," Sam said. "They seem to be leading me to the next step, to the next of the last 13. And I'm guessing that their job is to find whatever it is we need to win the race—some piece of the Bakhu, by the sounds of what Eva and Jedi were telling us."

"What did the piece of floor you took from Italy look like?" Xavier asked.

Sam thought about it. "Kinda like a gear from a bike, only it was brass, and the teeth were much smaller."

"Doesn't sound very Egyptian. Maybe da Vinci being the creator does make more sense. Although, the Egyptians did make some amazing stuff—"

"I'm pretty familiar with their pyramids," Sam smiled.

The two laughed as they remembered their climb up the Great Pyramid of Giza.

"That feels like ages ago already. Huh. You know, Ahmed took me on tours of some ancient Egyptian sites," Xavier said, "and through museum collections that he'd helped put together—researchers believe they may have even had power, like electricity, for lights and stuff."

"Really?" Sam said.

"Yep. Think about it—there aren't any torch marks inside the pyramids and tombs. The guys building them didn't use flaming torches when they were working in there, but something like the Baghdad Batteries."

"The what?" Sam's eyebrow's knit together in confusion.

"Here, like this," Xavier picked up his tablet and flicked to an image. He held it up for Sam to see.

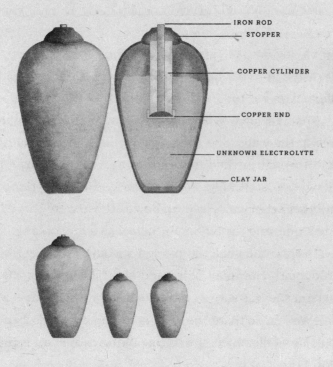

"Cool."

They were silent then, and when Sam started drifting off to sleep from sheer exhaustion, he was sure that Xavier was already talking in his sleep.

23

EVA

Eva lay awake, glad that Gabriella was asleep. Eva listened to her quiet snoring across the room, and she slipped on her robe and shoes and crept out of the door.

The hallway was dark, lit by a few small night lights set low in the walls. She went downstairs to the study rooms and through behind the gym to the science labs. There, beyond a "staff only" door at the end of a corridor, was another set of stairs leading down. These were carved into the stone, and the air down there was a lot cooler.

Despite the cold, the person she saw was wearing his trademark Hawaiian shirt and shorts. This was the one person she was sure would still be up at this hour—Jedi.

"Well, hello there," he said, standing in the kitchen area outside of his office. "I was just fixing myself an espresso. Want one?"

"No, thanks," Eva replied, shutting his office door behind her as they walked in. "I'll need to sleep at *some* stage tonight."

"Ah, sleep, I remember that," he said, taking his little cup over to his massive tri-screened workstation linked to an array of supercomputers in a vast room beyond a glass wall.

"How long have you been here, Jedi?" Eva asked after a while.

Jedi looked at his watch. "Oh, um, about twenty-one, twenty-two hours," he said.

"No," Eva laughed, "I meant, how long have you been at the Academy? How did you end up here?"

"Um, I didn't come by what you might call the 'traditional' route," Jedi hesitated and Eva nodded, silently urging him to go on. "My parents weren't Dreamers, or if they were, I didn't know it. My dad was a bit of a deadbeat and Mom wasn't much more use. So I started hanging out with other kids whose parents didn't care where they were. I skipped a lot of school, too much in the end, and got into all kinds of trouble, especially when it came to computers. Luckily the Academy found me in time."

He smiled and Eva was relieved to feel the tension in the room ease. "They showed me I could use my talents in other ways—even managed to make school cool!" He pretended to gasp in horror. Now he was laughing. "Stop looking so serious, Eva, my story has a happy ending and now I'm king of all I survey. Ah, Betsy . . ." Jedi swung his arms expansively around him.

Eva looked out the glass wall in front of her and gestured to Jedi's homemade supercomputer—his cluster of gaming consoles.

"And that would be Betsy?" Eva guessed.

"Yep! Isn't she a beauty?" his face beamed. "Over five thousand of them in there now, and for the next three hours we'll get our biggest worldwide connect of the day."

"I still don't know how that works," Eva confessed.

"And if the government ever asks you, that's your answer," Jedi said with a smile.

"Which government?" Eva said.

"Exactly!" he said, laughing. "That's the way. Now, watch this . . ."

He typed in some commands and there was a whirring sound as bank after bank of linked machines came online. Eva wasn't sure, but she thought the ceiling lights may have flickered—just a little.

"Hmm, she's chuggin' a bit of power," he said, sliding across on his chair to another console and tapping away furiously. "That should increase the Academy's geothermal energy output enough."

Eva settled into a chair as he slid back to his own console and started running programs.

"Right now, I'm tapped into millions of gamers online, running their consoles with my own . . ." Jedi's hands typed over the keyboard as fast and efficient as the most accomplished concert pianist. "That, in turn, makes Betsy a supercomputer with enormous crunching power."

"What are you searching *for*?" Eva asked.

"Right now, all things da Vinci—archives, collections,

documents and even just random mentions, just in case," Jedi tapped in a few more commands and chuckled to himself. "That's one of about two thousand searches I've set up to run tonight. Another focus is looking for anything we can use to help us understand more of the journal so we—hang on—ohhh . . ." A small bleep from another desk had stolen his attention.

He slid across to a lone computer, an ordinary looking laptop, and, in under two minutes, tapped in a page or so of type, mostly numbers and symbols. He then swivelled back to his command and control console, laughing and saying, "That'll keep him occupied for the next day or two."

"Him?" Eva raised a tired eyebrow.

"Matrix, my *nemesis*—I'll tell you about him another time," Jedi said, then sipped his coffee and kept chuckling to himself as he typed search queries.

"Are you able to identify any of the last 13 through your computers?" Eva asked.

Jedi shook his head as his eyes scanned his screens and he typed and clicked. "Nope," he said, taking another sip. "Could probably make a list of a thousand or so known Dreamers in the right age bracket, but there'd be no telling who the other remaining ten of the 13 are. That's what we need Sam for." Jedi coughed. "Would you like some water?"

"Please," Eva replied.

Jedi went over to his water dispenser and poured water into a couple of paper cups.

"Ten more to find, hey? Thank you," she said, accepting a cup and taking a sip. "You're counting Xavier with Sam and Gabriella? But Sam knows him from school. That doesn't make him the next of the 13, does it?" Eva said.

"Sam seems pretty determined to run around Germany with him, so I'm betting he's number three," Jedi reasoned.

"Has he dreamed of Solaris or anything specific for the prophecy?" Eva asked.

"Well, I mean—no, or maybe he has and he doesn't know it yet."

He's beginning to look uncomfortable with this conversation. What does he know?

"Do you have information on him?" Eva persisted.

"Who?" Jedi asked innocently.

"Xavier," Eva sighed.

"Oh yes, and his dad," Jedi said. "*Especially* his dad."

"Dr. Dark, the psychiatrist?" Eva said slowly.

"Yeah."

"He was my psychiatrist too," Eva said. "But you knew that, right?"

"Um, yeah," Jedi replied. "I might have read that some-place."

"Where? Do I have a file?" Eva asked.

"We all have files."

"Can I read it?"

"His file?" Jedi said. "Or your file?"

"His. And Xavier's. Mine—well, I don't know if I'm

ready for that just yet, about my parents I mean."

"Well, *I'm* not sure about a student accessing files . . ." Jedi hesitated.

"Or you could just tell me what you know about the last 13."

"I'd tell you that anyway," Jedi smiled.

"Yeah?"

"There's Sam, Gabriella, Xavier." Jedi crossed his arms in front of him. "Could be we know more of them . . ."

"I know what you're suggesting," Eva said, meeting his gaze.

"Alex, and you." Jedi did not flinch.

Eva shook her head. "We're like the other kids here. Nothing makes us part of the last 13."

"No, you're not like the others," Jedi said. "I'm not that big on coincidences and I don't believe it was just chance that the three of you were picked up by the Enterprise on the same day. And that Sam went to school with Xavier and you were seeing his dad, the shrink. Sorry," he added, seeing Eva wince at his last comment.

She looked away, conflicted and caught up in her thoughts. "Besides, Alex is dead—he was right underneath Sebastian's jet when it was shot down in New York," she said.

Jedi smiled again.

"What now?" she asked. "Tell me what that grin is for!" She started smiling herself, without even knowing why.

"It's because just before you got here, I found out," he said, tapping away and bringing up a photo of Alex date-stamped from the day before, "that Alex is still *very* much alive."

XAVIER'S NIGHTMARE

When I open my eyes, I'm swinging above a sea of green. *Am I in a jungle?*

I look down and realize I'm precariously balanced on the branch of a tree. Sam lies on the ground below me, moaning quietly.

Before I can call out to him, I hear a growl. The hairs on the back of my neck prickle.

There is movement in the shrubbery beneath me. A flash of orange, then it's gone.

What was ... was that a ... ?

Sam lifts his head and follows my gaze, staring fixedly toward the thick bushes. He forces himself up and limps to the tree, scrambling up to the first branch. I reach down to help him but as I look past him, I see huge yellow eyes watch us with savage curiosity.

It's a tiger. A big one. Where are we?

"I'm pretty sure they can climb trees," Sam whispers to me.

There is a noise, a grating sound, and the tiger turns its attention elsewhere. It's watching something unseen through the foliage, sniffs the air, and with a bound into the shrubbery, it's gone.

"Feeding time?" Sam says.

"Time to go," I say, forcing resolve into my voice.

"Xavier!" A voice is shouting from far off.

"Did you hear that?" I ask Sam. "Sounds like—"

"Xavier!"

"My dad!"

"Over here!" Dad calls out. He dangles a rope over an edge of the enclosure. We slide and drop our way down the tree and run the short distance to it. There are people yelling to us, urging us to climb. Hands reach out to help but they're too far above us to reach.

"Grab the rope and walk up the wall!" my father says. I've never seen such fear in his eyes. What is he afraid of? Then I realize. *He's scared for me* . . .

"You first," I say and hold the rope out for Sam. He goes hand-over-hand and walks his way up the rough cement-rendered wall. The minute that it takes ticks by agonizingly slowly. Sweat trickles into my eyes and I wipe my face with my sleeve.

"Xavier!" my father calls out.

I begin to climb. I hear the crowd's murmurings turn to shrieks and my panic rises like a wave, threatening to over-whelm me.

I look over my shoulder, the tiger is running toward me, readying to pounce.

I just manage to swing my legs from its reach but I'm slipping.

"Hang on!" Dad yells and wraps the rope around his forearm. He pulls backward, disappearing from view. Sam grabs onto the rope, other hands taking the strain with him, the rope running over the handrail and pulling me upward as—

"Argh!" I feel claws tearing at my leg as the tiger leaps toward me.

But suddenly I am on my back, heaving for air. *I thought I was a goner.*

I hear relieved sighs and exclamations all around me. My father leans over me, his eyes wet. *Is he crying? I've never seen him cry before . . .*

The massive brick and concrete tower reminds me of a medieval castle, only more modern and brutal in appearance.

We descend stairs—dank and dark—until we come to a concrete passageway that branches off in several directions.

"Which way?" my father asks.

"Follow me," I reply. A couple of turns later we come to a steel door. "Through there."

"What's through there?" Dad asks.

"What we came for," I reply. It's locked and we don't have the key. There's no budging it—this door is made to withstand more than a heavy push.

"There!" I say. There's an air duct built into the ceiling above us.

"There's no way that I—"

"Come on, Dad!" I say.

Sam leads with the help of a flashlight, and we wriggle our way through the confines of the duct, over the unyielding doorway and to the next grate. With a nudge of Sam's elbow, the grate pops free and falls downward with a splash.

"Great," Sam says, his voice echoing in the pitch dark.

"What is it?" I ask.

"It's flooded down there," he says.

"Keep taking the air duct?" I suggest. Sam shuffles ahead and sees that the duct drops off into a steep incline.

"Might be flooded too," he replies as we inch along for a better look. Before I can say or think anything else, we're skidding down the incline, our shouts of surprise echoing in the small space and making my ears ring.

I cough out water. I'm on my hands and knees, fighting for breath. I watch as a dark pool of water forms before me on the dry cement floor. Tears drip from my eyes.

For a few moments, I fight to regain my composure.

The light is dull and does not penetrate far, but I can make out a big warehouse-like cavern. I trace my way around, eventually finding a wall, which I follow until I fumble over a steel box, with big switches. I flick through them until I hear a thump, crack, spark, and then a loud humming.

Banks of lights switch on, flooding the space with blinding light, making me shade my eyes as they adjust.

I am standing, feet glued to the floor, mouth agape. Before me, an immense factory spreads out—a production line. Many of the shapes I cannot make out until I walk across the room and see the finished product. Several aircraft are lined up. They are without any markings or paint, simply aluminium and glass. Jet aircraft, no propellers. I move closer, standing under the nearest plane.

How can this be? Why is all this here?

"Xavier!"

I turn to see Sam and my father running toward me.

"RUN!" my father shouts.

BANG, BANG, BANG!

Bullets ricochet and spark off the machinery closest to me.

"Those German traitors!" Sam yells on his way past me.

I spin around and the world around me has changed. I'm still somewhere dimly lit, the atmosphere just as dank. I hear my own voice calling out weakly and struggle to move. Pain.

I'm on the ground. Bleeding.

"Sam," I say. "My father . . ."

"WHERE ARE YOU . . . ?"

The voice makes my blood run cold.

"Take this," I say, my voice weak, handing Sam a small brass disc.

"I'M GOING TO FIND YOU . . ." the voice comes from all around, everywhere at once.

"Don't let him get it," I say, and I can see Sam, sense a presence, but feel utterly helpless.

"I'm here too!" Sam is shouting, "I can see what you're seeing. C'mon we have to go!"

I can't move.

Another voice calls out to me—my father. I stand up to run toward him but he yells at me to stop.

"Go, Xavier, please! And always remember that I love you, son," he says.

I smile, "I love you t—"

I hesitate at a movement behind him. Within the darkness of the shadows, there's something even darker, and before I can say another word, fire erupts out of the dark, engulfing my father and coming straight toward me.

Sam is screaming, "Noooo! Xavier! Xavier, wake up!"

And I'm screaming too, and then I close my eyes.

There's only me now.

SAM

"Noooo!"

Sam sat up in bed, panting for breath. There were sounds from across the room—Xavier was still asleep but murmuring fitfully.

"Xavier!" Sam watched him violently toss and turn in his sleep as though he were trying to fight someone. "Xavier, wake up!"

Xavier continued to thrash in his bed and then screamed.

Dr. Dark came running in and shook his son awake. "Xavier! It's me, Dad, wake up, son!"

Xavier's eyes flew open and he sat up abruptly, looking from his father to Sam, throwing his arms around his dad.

Sam got out of bed and paced the room. He was drenched with sweat, the bedsheets completely soaked through. That dream had been so vivid—the despair he'd felt was like a solid mass on his chest, he couldn't comprehend the others in the room with him.

"Sam—Sam, are you all right?" Dr. Dark asked.

"Yes," he replied, still pacing, until he saw Xavier's

face and he stopped. His friend seemed to be in an even worse state of shock.

He's one of the last 13 all right, and now he knows it for sure.

"I'm going to need some cool water and a washcloth," Dr. Dark said, more to himself than to Sam. He picked up the phone in the room and soon it was answered. He spoke into the receiver and hung up. "Otto's on his way."

Sam nodded.

"Sam, did Xavier say anything else before I came in here?" Dr. Dark asked as Xavier tried to calm himself.

"No," Sam replied. "He—*we*—had a nightmare."

Xavier looked at Sam, both of them understanding in that moment what had happened.

"We?" Dr. Dark looked from one boy to the other.

"Sam and I," Xavier said finally. "We were both there—we shared it."

"Sam, is that right?" Dr. Dark asked, amazement clearly showing on his face.

"I . . . I think so," Sam stammered. "If Xavier had the same dream about the tiger . . . and Solaris. And there were planes too, I think."

Xavier nodded slowly. "That was Solaris, wasn't it? It was so—and then he . . ." Xavier was still wide-eyed and trembling.

"Sam, if what you're saying is true, that you *shared* Xavier's dream . . . well, I've never heard of a Dreamer having such capabilities without extensive training, which

I'm sure you haven't received."

Sam shook his head and continued to pace the room.

Now I'm having other people's nightmares too? Oh man . . . don't freak out, breathe, breathe . . .

"In some ways we shouldn't really be surprised," Dr. Dark was saying to him. "You're the first Dreamer of the last 13, it seems quite possible that you'd be able to do such things intuitively."

The butler appeared at the doorway and Dr. Dark turned to him, "Thank you for coming so quickly, Otto," Dr. Dark said, moving toward him. "Could you please bring us some aspirin and arrange for—"

He stopped cold.

"What are you *doing?*" Dr. Dark asked.

The butler remained there, standing still, silent—then Sam noticed the gun comfortably gripped in his hand.

"My employer has a keen interest in these special Dreamers of yours," Otto said, his pistol pointed at Dr. Dark. "*And* what they will lead us to."

"Your *employer?*" Dr. Dark protested. "Do you mean *Hans?*"

"He has heard everything—there are ears everywhere," Otto pointed to the light switch, and Sam guessed there must be a tiny microphone in there, and in all of them, spread throughout the house.

"I don't believe this, how dare you threaten me!" Dr. Dark thundered. "Hans has been my friend for years!"

"Friendship has its limits," Otto said. He turned and looked down the hallway and smiled. Sam watched as another man stepped in from the shadows. He was squat and thick-set with a shiny bald head. Beside him loomed the unmistakable bulk of the German Guardians' leader.

"Ah, Dark, so good to see you again," the bald man said.

"Hans," Dr. Dark said, "what is the meaning of all this? Have you lost your mind?"

"You'll see soon enough," Hans replied, then turned to the Guardian and butler and said, "Get them cleaned up and bring them to the study."

Dressed and seated in an imposing study downstairs, the three captives sat opposite Hans as he turned his attention away from a laptop sitting in front of him. Two of the German Guardians stood sentry at the door.

Least I know who they're working for, that's one mystery solved. Information that would have been more helpful yesterday, though.

"So, Xavier . . ." Hans said. "I've not seen you since you were much younger, how have you—"

"Yeah? Can't say that I've missed you," Xavier blurted out.

Sam smiled. Xavier was sounding like his old self again.

"And Sam," Hans said, ignoring Xavier and wagging his finger at Sam. "Sam, I have not yet met. You are a curiosity. Very, very interesting indeed . . ."

"Pleasure's all yours," Sam said.

"Hmph, some manners they have, these boys of yours, Dark," Hans said.

"What can I say?" Dr. Dark replied. "They know a rat when they see one. Why are you doing this?"

"I've been after this treasure as long as you have," he replied. "And now it's really happening, after all these years . . . and these *kids* are going to lead me to it." Hans tapped the rolled-up paper of the Stele rubbing sitting on his desk.

"Treasure?" Sam said. "You're selling out your friend, all of us, *for treasure?*"

"Sure, why not? Besides, I'm not *selling out* a friend," Hans said. "We've helped each other out over the years, and now he's helped me to get to the two of you—and *you'll* lead me to what I want. Although I could hardly have imagined that you would deliver them right to me!" he sniggered at Dr. Dark.

Dr. Dark glowered in return, looking as if he was ready to strangle Hans with his bare hands. "You know it's not treasure that lies at the end of this, Hans," Dr. Dark said. "It's not gold or diamonds or whatever you've dreamed up might be there. There's no Aladdin's cave."

"It's 'the greatest treasure of our ages,' Dr. Dark, and

that goes beyond your crummy theories of the 'treasure of the mind' and all that psychological garbage," Hans said, standing to light a cigar and then sitting on the edge of his desk. "You see, I've listened in on everything you said in this house, and if da Vinci thought it was so important, and went to such lengths to conceal the treasure, it's *monumental*—much, much more incredible than I ever imagined. And it will make me the most powerful man in the world. I can think of lots of things I'd like to do with that much power."

Dr. Dark had fury burning in his eyes.

"Come now. Your mock outrage is really quite naive," Hans said, breaking into a huge grin. He turned his attention back to Sam and Xavier, "So, did you boys have a good dream? Judging by the look of you when you woke, it must have been exciting stuff, eh? Time for you to tell Uncle Hans all about it."

"And why would we do *that*?" Xavier spat.

"Because otherwise you might find yourself unexpectedly promoted to the head of the Dark Corporation," Hans said, pulling out a revolver and pointing it at Dr. Dark. Sam grabbed Xavier's arm to restrain him as he leapt out of his seat at Hans. *Not now, Xavier . . . choose your battles.*

"I have your attention, I see. So tell me—what's the next step in our little treasure hunt?"

EVA

E va still couldn't sleep. She was in bed, the room dark, Gabriella's quiet snoring a comfort. Somehow.

I should record it, release it on the Internet as her latest hit song . . .

Eva smiled and rolled onto her side.

How could Jedi think Alex and I were part of the last 13? And if Alex was and now he's gone off somewhere, what does that mean for the prophecy? Did Alex dream of Solaris and some piece of the Bakhu? Will I?

She adjusted the rubber skull cap that they wanted her to wear to record her dreams. The wires led under the bed to a recording device. *If I have my dream tonight, as one of the 13, then maybe Sam will come rushing back.*

She looked across the room at Gabriella, who'd so effortlessly had her own dream, which then led to the adventure in Rome. *No, not adventure—we were lucky to get out alive, all of us.*

Be careful what you wish for, her mother used to say. Enterprise Agents or not, Eva still missed her parents.

They'd *been* her parents in every sense—taking her to school, on holidays, all the things that regular parents did. Sure, she'd argued with them, but there was nothing, ever, that made her question their love for her.

At last, fitfully, slowly, Eva fell asleep.

Eva woke up cold and shaking.

It was still dark outside, she'd slept for maybe three hours. She sat up, her quilt wrapped around her shoulders, and pulled the dream cap off her head. She walked to the window. The first dull hues of dawn were starting to glow to the east—behind the mountain where she'd seen that fire.

The camp fire.

Eva squinted, searching for the tiny light she had seen. She struggled to recall what had woken her, but she knew there was a reason she had dreamed of that light.

Is someone trying to send me a message?

Images of the dream flicked through her mind, disjointed and broken. Hiking on the mountain, finding a camp, the ash of the fire and a room inside a cave.

Was that it? Is that where it ended?

The cave . . . the cave . . .

Try as she might, she couldn't remember. There was something about it, something that woke her, something important, but she couldn't recall it.

Maybe the dream recorder captured it? If it was a vivid enough dream, it would have been recorded.

Jedi.

Downstairs in the computing rooms, Jedi was nowhere to be seen. His bank of consoles was still rumbling and there was scrolling text flying down his screens at warp speed. Eva paced and waited for five, ten, fifteen minutes. She could wait no longer.

Gabriella still slept soundly in the bed on the other side of their room. Eva scribbled a note for her and left it next to her pillow.

Gabriella –

I've gone to hike out to the camp fire on the mountain.

Tell Lora I'll be back by tonight.

Tell her I dreamed I had to go, and I promise I'll be

careful. I've got my phone with me if she wants to call.

Eva

Eva set off in the crisp morning air to cross the mountain. She borrowed a snowmobile, figuring no one would mind and took the first leg at a flat-out pace, heading down the Academy's mountain, traversing along a flagged path that followed the main ridge line. The powder snow was easy going and it took her just twenty minutes to reach the point where she'd have to ditch the vehicle and go on foot—crossing a rocky pass and then hiking up the next mountain.

Dressed in snow clothes a couple of sizes too big—she couldn't find her size in the Academy's storeroom—Eva zigzagged her way up the steep mountainside, stopping at each turn to catch her breath as she exerted herself in the thin mountain air. The sun was peeking over the ridge now, bathing the Academy in light. They'd be awake any moment now, the students, staff, the Guardians. Maybe they'd be worried, but it was a clear bright day and she'd seen in her dream where she had to go.

I'll be fine, I'll be back for dinner.

"Next . . . time . . . though . . ." she said to herself, fighting for breath from the exertion, "I'm . . . gonna . . . work out . . . first."

Eva stopped and looked at the distance she'd covered and what lay ahead. It was going to be a long day.

Gabriella turned over in her bed, adjusting the eye mask over her eyes to shut out any tiny glimpse of the morning light. She felt the paper on her pillow wrinkle against her cheek as she rolled on it. In a half-awake daze, she lifted up one side of the sleep mask and reached for the note, skimming it quickly.

"Ergh, too cold to go hiking," she mumbled to herself, snapping the mask tight against her eyes again. She let the note fall from her grasp and it fluttered down, landing amongst piles of clothes and magazines on the floor. "And too *early*."

27

ALEX

Surprisingly, Alex did manage to sleep. In fact, no sooner had he taken a shower and texted Phoebe, than he felt a wave of sleepiness drifting over him. He just had time to lay down and pull the sheet up around his neck, and he drifted off. His last image was that of the Agent sitting across the room on his own bed, reading an army manual.

Alex groaned, rolled over and promptly fell out of bed with a bone-crunching *THUMP!*

"Ow!" he moaned as he pulled himself up and blinked as the room came into focus. *Where am I again?*

The grey wall decorated with two cheap modern art prints reminded him—the flight, the hotel in Berlin, his unhappy roommate . . . Alex spun around, banging his elbow on the bedside table next to him. "Oh man, are you kidding?" He rubbed his arm, getting up carefully to avoid any more brushes with furniture.

"So where's my new friend gone, huh?" he mused aloud. He checked in the adjoining bathroom but he was alone.

He picked up the phone to order some breakfast.

I need food . . . maybe some bacon . . . or ice cream. Huh? Ice cream? Ice cream! It was in my dream! Alex hung up the phone.

A deluge of images flashed through Alex's head and he sat down heavily on the bed, trying to bring into focus the kaleidoscope of pictures that streamed before his eyes. *Wait. Stop. What did I see?*

Alex took a deep breath, closed his eyes and sifted through the spiralling images. There were families all around. The sun was shining, kids laughing. It reminded Alex of Disney World, but the signs were different—the writing was different, it looked like German. There weren't any rides, but walkways and exhibits. Enclosures, even.

I'm in a zoo. A German zoo. OK, then what?

There were crowds of people and . . . *Stella?*

He'd followed her around the corner of a large brick building but it was a dead end. No one was there. There was a locked steel door marked *ACHTUNG!—POWER*. He'd tried the handle and somehow had gotten in.

It was dark but for the light coming through the half-closed door behind him. Ahead there were concrete stairs that led down, a grimy old light at the bottom. The murmuring of voices rose up to him. He'd followed them downstairs.

In the hotel room, Alex's eyes opened and he took a few deep breaths. It was scary just trying to remember what he'd dreamed. He felt elated and yet also fearful that he was now experiencing a true dream. And *remembering* it, this time.

He forced his eyes closed once more to concentrate.

Why is the zoo important? Is that where Sam is?

At the base of the concrete stairs there had been a cross tunnel that led left and right. The voices came from the left. The concrete floor had felt wet and slippery underfoot.

There had been an open door with light spilling out. He'd heard the voices, a woman's and a man's—at least, it was deep and low. But he was sure the female voice belonged to Stella. He'd leaned in to listen but they'd stopped talking. Silence. Then footfalls—*they're coming out!*

Alex had jerked back fast and in the process he'd slipped over and landed on his back. The breath had been knocked out of him. Above him stood Stella.

Behind her . . . behind her . . .

Alex's eyes flew open again. He grimaced with the effort to recollect the end of the dream. What had they been saying? *Did I hear them in the original dream? Doesn't matter, now I know where to go.*

"You're sure?" Phoebe said to Alex.

"No doubt," Alex said.

"And Stella and her team are headed there now?"

"Yes."

"OK, stay near your phone and I'll see what I can find out and call you back."

"OK, thanks . . . Mom."

"Be safe, Alex."

He hung up and looked again at the note he'd just found taped to the back of the door—*Stay here.*

"Stay here, my butt," Alex said, scrunching up the paper and tossing it on the Agent's bed. He slung his backpack over his shoulder and left the room, headed downstairs, where he spoke to the receptionist to find out when his group had left— two hours ago.

A bit of a head start, then . . . well, I'm not waiting around here to lose any more time.

Alex had the concierge call him a cab and waited impatiently outside the hotel.

If his mother called with different information, he'd change his plans. But right now he'd had a true dream and he trusted it.

A cab promptly pulled up and Alex got in and promised the driver a generous tip if he could get him to the zoo in record time. The tires squealed as they pulled away into the Berlin traffic.

28

SAM

Sam and Xavier wasted no time in telling Hans a fantastical tale about Xavier's dream—a building in Madrid with a red sign outside, a room with a broken window and a box with something important inside. Once Xavier warmed up to his subject, his creative juices had really started to flow. Hans swept out of the room to investigate, leaving two German Guardians to watch them.

Is he really falling for this? How are we going to get out of here before he works out we're lying to him?

"Why'd you sell us out?" Sam asked the Guardian closest to him. "Why'd you turn?" Here, finally, was his chance to find out why the Guardians had proven to be so disloyal.

"He won't tell you anything, Sam," Dr. Dark said. "But it's clear he favours country over cause."

"Or money," Xavier added.

The Guardians remained silent.

Sam looked down at his Stealth Suit. *If only I could figure out how to change it into something tough or slippery, to give me just enough of an advantage.*

And he could hardly ask Dr. Dark for help—even if he knew how to control the suit, the Guardians would be on him before he could blink.

Maybe the Stealth Suit would react if I was under threat? Maybe if my survival was at stake, it'd change to help me? No—surely that would have happened a few times by now.

The minutes crept by painfully slowly—it felt like hours to Sam, but Dr. Dark looked as if he was calmly sitting in a waiting room for an appointment. *I guess that's where Xavier gets his super coolness from, huh?*

"We have to get out of here," Sam whispered to them both, "before Hans works out what we've done."

A Guardian poked him hard with the tip of his gun. "No talking."

And so it went every time they tried to start up a conversation. The minutes turned into an hour, then two. Sam thought Xavier had fallen asleep when . . . he seemed to be signalling something with his eyes.

The fireplace?

Sam mouthed, "*What?*"

But Xavier played it cool as a Guardian shifted positions closer to him.

Sam saw a pile of logs next to the fire and a steel bucket holding packs of firelighters. Sam shuddered to think what Xavier was thinking of doing with it . . . *I'm not good with fire, Xav,* but before he could even second-guess him—

Xavier was out of his chair and headed for the fire and the two Guardians sprang into action, rushing at him.

Dr. Dark was up in a flash and crash-tackling the closest one.

The other drew his dart gun and fired at Xavier, the barbed needles spitting forth as quickly as he could pull the trigger, the shots hitting the stone hearth and zeroing in on Xavier as—

Sam swept out a kick that floored the Guardian, taking him completely off guard. He leapt to his feet and sprang backward as the Guardian reached for him. Sam punched his arm away then followed up with a cupped hand impacting against the Guardian's jaw, hitting a nerve that instantly knocked him out.

Sam swung around to take in the scene behind him.

The second Guardian had given Dr. Dark a bloodied nose and gotten to his feet, rushing at Xavier. A burst of fire erupted as Xavier pushed the logs off the fire out onto the rug-covered parquet floor, then he tipped out a packet of firelighters.

WHOOSH!

The inferno was instant and immense. The Guardian raised his fist to Dr. Dark.

SMASH!

Sam broke his chair across the meaty back of the Guardian. The huge hulk stopped in his tracks. He turned, his eyes and anger only for Sam now.

Uh-oh!

He staggered toward him, and as he neared—

THWACK! THWACK!

Two darts drilled into the guy's chest.

Dr. Dark was lying on the ground, grasping the unconscious Guardian's weapon.

"Sweet dreams," he said, and then Sam ducked out of the way as the Guardian fell forward and landed with an almighty crash.

"That was pretty awesome, Xavier!" Sam smiled to his friend.

"Well, I was getting bored sitting around. Those guys were no fun," he grinned.

"Too right! Let's get out of here," Sam said, as Xavier helped his father to his feet.

"How?" Xavier asked.

"Make for the car?" Sam said as he dived across the desk to snatch up the rubbing of the Dream Stele. *Hans is going to kick himself for leaving this in here.* Sam allowed himself a malicious chuckle.

"Sam's right, we have to get to a car," Dr. Dark said, running to the door and locking it.

"What about the fire?" Sam said, trying not to show his fear of the flames that were now licking across the floor.

Loud banging hammered at the door and made them all jump.

"They'll deal with it," Dr. Dark said, as the banging gave way to heavy ramming from the other side. "Quick, out the window!"

In the garage they found Arnold dozing in the Mercedes, blissfully ignorant of the dramatic events of the last few hours. He nearly had a heart attack when Dr. Dark yanked the passenger door open.

"Arnold," Dr. Dark said, "head east and make them chase you for as long as they can!"

"Yes, boss!" Not needing to be told any more, Arnold started the car, revved the engine and skidded down the sweeping driveway, gravel flying up behind.

"What do we do now?" Sam asked

Dr. Dark smiled. "We drive south."

Sam had thought just yesterday that he'd never be in such a fast car again. Turned out he was wrong—this time, they were driving even faster. Dr. Dark had Hans' Porsche 911 Turbo topped out at nearly three hundred kilometres per hour.

"At least we know why the German Guardians were in your nightmare, Xav," Sam said with a scowl. "They're working for Hans now."

"I'm taking you boys to the Academy," Dr. Dark said. "We'll take the next exit and then stick to the back roads.

They'll be watching the airports, expecting us to get out the fastest way."

"This is pretty fast," Sam said. He felt dizzy watching cars blur past the window.

"But what if they work out where to go next before we do?" Xavier said.

"How could they do that?" Dr. Dark asked, puzzled.

"Well, turns out it's close to here," Xavier said.

"It's back in Berlin," Sam added.

Dr. Dark eased off the accelerator and then pulled the car over to the emergency lane of the autobahn before he took the turnoff ahead. Cars flashed by at warp speed. Ahead of them the road split. One road headed south, eventually to Switzerland and the safety of the Academy; the other westward, to Berlin and to their dreamed future.

"Tell me," Dr. Dark said. "Tell me more about your night-mare."

"Well, first I thought I was in a jungle . . ." Xavier recounted his dream, up to the appearance of Solaris and the fire. He hesitated, stopped short by the horror of his dream, the crushing feeling of emptiness, of losing his father in the inferno that Solaris had created.

"Solaris really is here now. I saw him in Italy, two nights ago," Sam said. "I had to fight him."

"You fought him?" Dr. Dark said in amazement.

"Yes." Sam winced at the memory.

"And lived to tell the tale. What did he look like?"

"Full mask, maybe some kind of advanced Stealth Suit," Sam said. "He's tall, strong, quick. Shoots fire from his wrists and shows no mercy."

"But he's certainly no incarnation of some unbeatable evil," Dr. Dark said, almost as if he were trying to convince himself.

Sam noticed something in the doctor's demeanour.

Is it fear?

Sam said, "You've seen him, too, haven't you?"

Dr. Dark grimaced. "No, but my childhood nightmares were plagued by a fearsome presence—the Professor too, and Jack, we later found out. It's part of the curse of these dreams. The deeper you go into the dream world, the less you can control who steps out of the shadows."

He glanced at Sam and Xavier, who looked scared.

"But it's just a dream," Dr. Dark reassured. "I don't believe in some sinister bogeyman from ancient prophecies coming to life—here and now, in this day and age. It's trickery, nothing more, someone out to spook you into making mistakes."

Sam thought back to the first time he thought he'd confronted Solaris in the subway station beneath the museum. He'd discovered upon unmasking him that it was Stella, the rogue Agent from the Enterprise. But that figure he'd met in Rome was certainly not her—it was, in every detail, how he'd dreamed Solaris to be.

"So we have no choice," Dr. Dark said, dropping the

clutch and flooring the Porsche. "We must get to Berlin before anyone else—Hans and those traitorous German Guardians, Solaris, whoever. We must beat them to it."

Sam looked to Xavier as his father took the Porsche toward its top speed again. They both knew that there was another detail that they'd not shared—that Dr. Dark had been killed by Solaris. There was a look in Xavier's eyes that begged Sam not to bring up that fact just yet. Sam wordlessly agreed, but his gut told him that try as they might, being as careful and quick as they could, lives would be at risk that day.

At the Berlin Zoo, the park had not long been open and throngs of people were queuing up to get through the gates.

"I'm going to drive around the block and find a spot for us to wait. We'd be too vulnerable waiting in line," Dr. Dark said.

Sam and Xavier were silent. They'd been in the city for over an hour, during which time they'd refuelled the car and gotten some breakfast. Dr. Dark had heard from Arnold that the diversion had not worked—after some ten minutes of being pursued, the three Porsche SUVs which had been on his tail had disappeared. Until he knew where they were, Sam could see that Dr. Dark would be anxious.

"I don't like it . . ." Dr. Dark said. "It doesn't feel right."

They drove around the back of the zoo and then had to wait for a traffic light to change.

Dr. Dark drummed his fingers on the dashboard. Xavier looked ill and uneasy at the prospect of what might happen now that they were at the site of his dream.

And Sam was looking out the windows of the car, alert, watching for—

"Look!" he said. "Across the road, on the left!"

The three silver Porsche SUVs sat at the intersection. Their light turned green.

"Hang on!" Dr. Dark floored the accelerator and the sports car flew off the mark, weaving an illegal path through the morning's traffic.

"How'd they find us?" Xavier asked.

Dr. Dark shook his head.

"There must be a tracking device somewhere on this car," Sam said.

"Darn it!" Dr. Dark said. "Of course, you're right."

He fell silent as he flew through an intersection against the traffic light. Behind them, a bus pulled out in front of their pursuers, and Sam was happy to see them stalled in a cloud of brake dust and tire smoke.

"OK, change of plans," Dr. Dark said. "I'll drop you two at the gate. Hide in the crowd and get in as fast as you can."

"No, Dad . . ." Xavier began.

"Blend in, stick to a tour group," Dr. Dark continued. "If it looks too dangerous, stay low and hide, don't go taking stupid risks, got it?"

"It's better this way," Sam said, his hand on Xavier's shoulder to get his attention, and his friend nodded. *At least then that part of his nightmare can't come true, right?*

Dr. Dark said, "Call me when you're out."

"But they might catch you," Xavier protested.

Dr. Dark smiled.

"No. They won't," he said, and Sam believed him. "I'll lead the chase all over town, and in that time you'll get whatever it is you need. If it gets too dangerous for me, I'll stop in front of a police station and run inside."

They pulled up to the zoo's main entry gates once more.

"Go!" Dr. Dark said. "And good luck!"

Inside the zoo, Sam and Xavier attached themselves to a guided tour headed for the carnivore house.

"Wow, nice zoo," Xavier said lookimg about the grounds as they walked in the middle of some fifty tourists. "Hey, so how come in the dream, it was like we were in the zoo from years ago, not today?"

"I honestly don't know. My first dream was just as it happened in New York, and Gabriella's dream, or what I saw of it, was here and now too," Sam said. "I checked on my notebook on the drive in and that factory hasn't been in use since the Second World War. I guess our dreams aren't restricted by time and space," Sam shrugged.

"Cool . . ." Xavier grinned. "Bits of the zoo still kind of look the same though. I guess some parts didn't change during the war—hey look, in my dream, that's where we went through." Xavier pointed to the carnivore house up ahead. "Inside, past the tiger enclosure, then down into the basement level, some kind of a nocturnal animal area, along a few old corridors—and the air duct—and then we end up in the underground factory, full of aircraft parts."

"Exactly," Sam agreed.

"You know they were World War Two aircraft parts?" Xavier said. "I'm sure I saw some Messerschmitt Me 262s. They were the world's first jet fighter aircraft—really mean machines."

"Is there anything you *don't* know?" Sam jibed.

"I'm a bit of a nerd for model airplanes," Xavier admitted. "Dad too—he would have loved to see them. Hey, don't go telling kids at school I build models, I have my cool image to maintain," he chuckled.

"I don't think you have to worry about our old school anymore," Sam replied. "Besides, no one thought you were cool, just really rich and super smart and annoying."

"Annoying?" Xavier said, pretending to be offended.

"Little bit. Probably because you're super rich and really smart," Sam laughed. "And a little annoying."

"I thought it was super—ah, doesn't matter," Xavier said. "Anyway, your grades are as good as mine, sometimes better."

"Yeah, but I have to work like ten times harder than you do to get them."

"Not true," Xavier said, looking down at his feet as they

neared the carnivore enclosure. "You've got no idea how many tutors Dad has over at the house, making sure I ace every test. Practically every night, and . . . I haven't had a school holiday since fifth grade."

"What?" Sam was stunned.

"Dad organizes classes for me, so the holidays are just like normal school days," Xavier sighed.

"Oh man, sorry. I didn't know," Sam said, feeling bad for his classmate who'd now become his friend. "I guess he's into the whole 'nature/nurture' thing. I'm sure he was only trying to do his best for you."

"Yeah, I suppose."

"Look, for what it's worth, I used to think your dad was a bit full-on, but it seems like he's chilled out a bit now. This whole thing of you being a Dreamer, perhaps it's changing him, eh?"

"Yeah, maybe . . . he does seem a bit different," Xavier said. "Like he's got more confidence in me, more trust."

"He was probably pushing you so hard through school because he knew that one day this might happen, right?" Sam reasoned. "You'd be a Dreamer, maybe one of the last 13, using your wits, your mind, to beat huge armed guys and trained Agents. So really, it's like you've just been well prepared."

Xavier nodded. The tour guide stopped the group before entering the carnivore house and was talking, in English, about the history of the exhibit.

"Any questions before we go further?" the guide asked.

"Yes," Sam said, getting to the front of the group. "Is there a large tower near here?"

"Tower?" the guide said.

"Yeah, like a big concrete thing, maybe ten storeys tall?"

The guide laughed and shook his head. "Not anymore," he said. "You are probably referring to the 'Zoo Tower,' built in the Second World War to defend against air attacks. It's long gone now—the British Army blew it up after the war ended. Where the tower was is now our hippo-potamus park."

"OK, thanks," Sam said, and the guide ushered the group on, Xavier and Sam falling into step behind.

"It's time to ditch this group and begin our search," Sam said, pointing at a blue sign above them.

"And not a moment too soon," Xavier said, grabbing Sam's arms and breaking into a run as he motioned over his shoulder at Hans and his German Guardians, who were pushing through the crowds looking for them. "Let's get out of here before they spot us," he whispered, pulling Sam toward the flight of stairs ahead of them.

30

Sam and Xavier flattened themselves against the wall of the staircase as a Japanese tour group crowded up the stairs. Gently pushing against the tide of people, they slipped downward to the animal house below. The high-pitched squeaks of bats greeted them as they pushed farther in.

"Where now?" asked Sam. "There was an access panel above a steel door in the dream, is that how you remember it?"

"Yep, and I know just where to go. C'mon, follow me," Xavier replied. He confidently wove his way through the exhibit. Sam caught sight of an owl behind the glass next to them, but then it was gone as they jogged along, the other animals a blur on either side.

Xavier stopped suddenly, turning around, looking for something. "It should be near here, maybe back around the last corner." They retraced their steps for a moment, Xavier searching for something. "This is it!" he said, excited. He walked up to a door with *"Mitarbeiter Nur"* on it and tried the handle.

"I'm guessing this is a staff area, right?" Sam said as he stood close to Xavier, both of them shielding the handle from the view of passing tourists. Sam inserted the blade of his pocket knife between the door and frame and jiggled it, trying to dislodge the lock. "Well, you never know when you might need a knife," Sam said in reply to Xavier's stare.

There was a quiet click and the door cracked open. They grinned at each other as they slipped inside.

The space was now clearly a storeroom, with equipment and boxes filling the small space. Xavier walked to the back of the room and shoved a large shelf to the side. "Look! Here's the door," he said.

"Except now it's even more impossible to get through it," Sam sighed, looking at the years of dirt and rust all over it. "And we still don't have a key."

"But, we *do* know how to get around it," Xavier beamed. He pointed out the access panel in the ceiling above and they began dragging boxes underneath it to create a make-shift ladder.

"Think Solaris will show?" Xavier asked as they squeezed along the air duct.

"All of this looks pretty much as we dreamed it so far, so it's a real possibility," Sam replied, leading the way with his flashlight.

"OK, this is it, hang on." Sam prised his pocket knife into a seam of the duct and twisted and turned the blade until he had made a hole in the connecting seam.

"This way, we don't have to do the waterslide part of our dream," Sam said, lifting out the panel and then shining the light down—"OK, well, it looks like it's a decent drop."

"Define *decent*," Xavier said.

"Maybe three metres, so make sure you bend your knees on landing, and roll out of it."

"Yeah, sure," Xavier said. "I'll just pull a few years of judo out of my pocket so I can have landing skills like you."

"It's not judo, it's—" Sam went out legs first, felt them dangling down in the air below, "—jujitsu."

Drop. Bend. Roll.

"Ah, OK, it's closer to four metres!" Sam's voice echoed up. He shone his light up at Xavier's dangling legs, watching as he hung on right to the end of his fingertips before letting go and landing in a big crash and grunt of pain. Sam couldn't help but laugh.

"Yeah, laugh it up, buddy," Xavier said, getting to his feet and dusting himself off. "I'd like to see Hans do that."

"Yeah, well, they must find another way in, no way those Guardians could fit through *that*," Sam said, pointing to the duct above them. "Come on."

"I'll get the lights," Xavier said, moving over to a row of switches on the wall opposite.

"No, wait," Sam said, smiling. "Leave it dark."

"Huh?"

"Think about it—we know where we're going because we've been here before in your dream," Sam said. "So let's just use our flashlights, and leave Hans and his goons in the dark."

"I like it," Xavier smiled.

Sam and Xavier ran side-by-side, trusting their recall of the dream. They rounded the corner and stopped dead in their tracks. Before them, a cavernous space stretched out into the darkness. They ventured inside, and soon, by their flashlights, the ghostly shapes of massive aircraft, heavy machinery and weapons parts were revealed, all of them covered in decades of dust.

"When do you think someone was last in here?" Xavier whispered. "This place is amazing. Look!" He ranged his light over the ancient planes, marvelling at the vintage aircraft.

"We have to get past the finished aircraft," Sam said. "Wherever they are."

"And right here is where—" Xavier said.

KLAP-BOOM!

They froze as an immense explosion resounded from the far end of the factory, echoing throughout the concrete bunker, the shock wave sending a cloud of dust billowing up against them and engulfing everything in a thick fog.

"Hans must have blasted his way in!" Sam said, coughing against the dust and pulling his Stealth Suit up over his mouth and nose to filter the air. "Let's move!"

"I can't see!" Xavier cried out.

"Hang on to the back of my shirt," Sam said.

Sam felt his way forward, moving slowly around huge steel machines that formed the assembly line. *At least Hans and his Guardians can't see in this either!*

"Wait," Xavier said. "Turn right here—there should be stairs leading up."

In the settling dust, Sam could see the rungs of rusted steel stairs and Xavier took the lead as they raced upward. As they went, they broke through the low-lying dust cover and saw that the stairs led up to a box-like office, the size of a large room in a house. The office was suspended over the production line by a series of steel rails that hung from the ceiling, enabling the whole structure to be moved around to hover over any area of the vast warehouse below.

"I could use a little help!" Xavier said at the top of the stairs.

Sam climbed up to stand next to him at the closed metal door, stuck tight into its frame. Together, with two, then three heavy bumps from their shoulders, the door burst inward.

Inside, the air was clear. The room held a few desks and chairs, drawing boards and filing cabinets. Glass windows ran all along the two long walls that looked up and down the long expanse of the warehouse, while the shorter side walls were solid metal panelling.

Sam cranked a lever set next to the door that retracted

the metal stairs from the floor and shut the door, cursing the noise that it made.

"Cover your light," Sam said, as he smothered his own with his free hand so it became just a dull glow. From out the windows, they could see several sets of powerful flashlights coming from the farthest end of the factory. "They're going to be slowed down thanks to their dust cloud, so we've got maybe a couple of minutes. We have to work fast. But I didn't see this in my earlier dream—only the planes and you, holding a Gear in your hand."

"Way ahead of you," Xavier said, and in the darkness of the office he worked his way around the several desks. "This is what we need."

Sam came closer and could see Xavier's flashlight shining on a small brass wheel attached to the wall.

"Is that . . . ?" Sam said.

"The Gear?" Xavier said. "No. Look." He waved his arm over a panel of buttons and dials, caked with dust, dull and corroded from years of neglect. Next to it was a simple switch. "It's the control panel for the office. Let's hope it still works." Xavier moved closer to the wheel and gave it a half turn counter-clockwise. He stood there, waiting, expectant.

Sam said, "Was something supposed to—"

"Look!" Xavier pointed to the ceiling above them.

A long row of red flashing lights had blinked on, illumi-nating a pulley system that spanned the length of the factory, set high into the ceiling.

CLINK, CLINK, CLINK!

"Um, what's happening?" Sam said, hanging onto a desk for stability as the whole room started to move, achingly slow, across the workshop floor.

"It's taking us where we need to go!"

The control room trundled across to the other side of the massive factory and stopped when it butted up against the solid concrete wall opposite. Problem was, they were now almost on top of Hans' advancing party.

As the control room came to rest, Xavier went to the wall next to a cabinet and felt around the metal panelling, his hands flat against the surface, rubbing lightly, feeling around for—

CLICK!

The wall had a hidden door panel, which opened into the room.

"Whoa!" Sam whispered.

"Cool, huh?" Xavier grinned. They looked into the dark tunnel, barely a metre wide and two metres tall, which formed a perfect hole of inky blackness that their lights could barely penetrate.

"Ah, Xavier?" Sam said.

"It's in there," Xavier said, standing at the threshold.

"Then why are we waiting here?"

"I . . . this part of my dream was scary," Xavier's smile vanished.

"Scared of the dark?"

"No, just . . . I never told you how I lost my mom, did I?"

Sam shook his head, waiting for him to go on.

"You know how you made that joke about being a secret agent? Well, my mom—she actually *was* one. Worked for the CIA, or some covert part of it, anyway. I didn't know that until after she'd died, when my father thought I was old enough to hear the truth. She . . . died . . . on a mission, doing stuff just like this. It took me so long to even forgive her for leaving us. All I ever wanted after that was to keep me and my dad safe. Now look what we're doing! And I don't even know if my dad is OK . . ." his eyes filled with sadness and anger.

Sam took Xavier by the shoulders and shook him gently. "I hear what you're saying but this is your destiny now. And what your mom would have wanted for you. I promise that we'll stick together and we'll get through this, OK?"

Xavier blinked furiously, pushing away tears and wiped his arm across his face. "I know you're right, but this is full-on . . . who knew that . . ."

PLINK!

A dart struck the glass window from an assailant down below.

"Man, we gotta go!" Sam said. "Come on!"

Xavier nodded as he plunged into the darkness. He led the way, setting off down the tunnel at a run, Sam's foot-falls sounding close behind him. He slowed as they passed signs on the walls, written in red paint. Even in German, the liberal use of exclamation marks left no doubt that they were ominous warnings of what might be up there.

"It should be close." Xavier stopped abruptly and Sam bumped into him. The tunnel ahead suddenly ended and in its place was the same solid concrete wall as those to his left and right.

"It's a dead end," Sam said.

"No, it's not," Xavier replied, and banged his feet. A hollow sound rang out. They shone their flashlights down. Underfoot was a thick metal plate. "You get that side."

Together they put their hands into two rusted handles and heaved open the trap door, resting it back against the wall.

"That looks like . . ." Sam trailed off. Below the trap door was another, only this one was round, concave and with a huge wheeled handle to turn.

"A submarine hatch," Xavier said, grinning. "I thought so too, when I saw it in my dream. They must have used a surplus hatch when they built this place during the war. I mean, why not use it? It's the perfect door to seal out water and pressure, to keep what's beyond it safe, right?"

"Right."

"On three," Xavier said, and they knelt down to the

ground and counted.

"Wait!" Sam said. "All those warning signs leading in here—maybe there's something dangerous under this hatch."

"No, it's fine," Xavier reassured.

"Really?" Sam worried.

"Really. You all right?"

"Yeah. You, ah, dreamed this, right? Whatever is under this hatch?"

"A giant squid from outer space," Xavier said deadpan.

Sam smiled. "Nothing we can't handle then."

"Right. On three." They counted again and then heaved with all their strength to open the wheel—to no avail. "Oh, it's the other way. We have to turn it counter-clockwise, like that one back at the control room."

On three the wheel started to turn.

And turn, and turn, until—

HISS . . .

It opened upward. Beyond, a ladder led down to a steel mesh floor a few metres below.

"After you," Sam said.

Xavier didn't need encouragement, he was down the ladder quicker than Sam could blink, and he followed.

"Oh boy . . ." Sam said.

They were in a storage room, full of wooden boxes. Sam could see that they were labelled in German.

"This one is full of books," Xavier read from a box then

stopped at a dusty inventory list clipped to the wall near the ladder. "And this one," he pointed to another, "has artifacts of significance . . . this one is art, this one scientific papers . . ." he continued to point out various boxes around them.

"You can read German?" Sam said, as Xavier scanned through the list. "Of course you read German. I mean, who doesn't, right?"

Xavier tapped the list. "This is it—Operation New Swabia. Aisle C, crate 12."

"C12," Sam said, leading the way and heading two rows down to the junction that spliced through the aisles. "You've sunk my battleship."

Xavier tried to smile, letting go of his sadness once more.

That's right, Xav. Get back into the here and now. But wow, what a story about his mom . . .

He counted off the numbered crates as he walked past them.

"These crates sure didn't get in here through *that* hatch," he said, pointing above them.

"I know," Xavier replied. "There must be another access point."

"A *big* one," Sam said, and then stopped. He shone his flashlight at a crate marked "12," along with one word.

"'*Antarktische*'?" Sam said.

"Antarctica."

"The Germans sent an expedition to Antarctica during the war?" Sam asked.

"Looks like it."

The bang of an explosion echoed through the chamber.

"What was *that*?" Xavier said.

"Sounded like a stun grenade. Maybe they're at the control room now, trying to flush us out."

"Then we'd better hurry before they realize we're not in there and come looking for us down here."

"Grab the other side," Sam said, and they dragged the washing machine-sized crate out into the aisle, broke the tape seals and undid the latches. They popped off the wooden lid.

"Ah . . . Xavier?" Sam said, looking at the contents. "I hope you're right about this."

Several gas masks stared up at them. Sam pulled them out to find the next layer was made up of large lead cubes, with U235 stencilled on the sides.

"Are you sure this is it?" Sam said, looking around them, trying not to touch anything with his hands.

New rule . . . if I don't know what it is, I don't touch it.

"Maybe there's another crate. I mean, they all look the same."

"This is it, I'm sure," Xavier said. "This stuff is important —important enough to be kept here while waiting for submarine transport someplace."

"How do you know that?" Sam asked, holding his

flashlight so that Xavier could keep unpacking the crate.

"That's how it was listed on that inventory list."

Xavier carefully put the contents of the well-stacked crate aside until finally he pulled out a flat wooden box, the size of a CD cover. Xavier stood back, popped the clasp, and despite the darkness Sam could make out the gleam of the bright brass Gear. They'd found the next piece of the Bakhu.

We're another step closer.

EVA

Eva had drained three of her four water bottles and eaten all but one of the energy bars she'd packed. She sat on her backpack on a wide ledge at the base of a sheer cliff. Above her there was maybe another hour's climb. Her legs burned, her face was numb and she was short of breath.

The sun now beamed back at her, perched on the other side of the Academy, blinding her as she trekked through the bright-white snow. Her ski goggles were tinted, but gave a weird distortion of the world underfoot and blocked her peripheral vision as she climbed onward.

What was worse, with maybe only three hours of decent sunlight left until it disappeared behind the other side of the Academy's taller mountain. It would be sunset a couple of hours after that, she was running out of time.

She contemplated calling the Academy—had Gabriella found her note? She looked down at the phone in her shaking hands and saw that it was struggling to find reception. One lowly bar flickered on and off on the screen. She smiled wryly. *Maybe I should have asked Jedi for a phone upgrade too?*

Eva was sure Lora and the Professor would understand her being out here, if it meant finding out about her dream. What was it Lora had once said to her about Sam going it alone to follow his dreams? *"It's not a perfect situation . . . but a necessary one."*

She willed herself to get moving again. To the side, it looked as though she'd shave off half the time if she was strong enough to make a near vertical ascent as a short-cut. From up there, where she'd seen the fire, maybe she'd be able to see a clear way back, a quicker way not visible from the pass. She banged her crampons free of ice and frozen snow, strapped them tightly back onto her boots and stood to set off.

Eva checked her watch again—another hour had slipped by. She was closer to her goal now after summoning the strength to make the more challenging vertical climb.

Maybe I'm not as unfit as I thought I was. Trying out for the track team has finally paid off. If only Mr. Lawson at school could see me now, ha!

She pulled off her backpack and dug around for a water bottle. She ran her tongue over her cracked lips and realized how sunburnt she had become. "Where *is* that bottle?" she mused to herself as she rummaged in the bag.

She paused for a moment as she heard a noise. It

sounded like a wave at the beach. She stood still, listening.

Is that a plane?

"Where is that coming from—?"

She looked up, too late.

An avalanche.

There wasn't even enough time to panic as a wall of blinding whiteness threw itself on Eva, picking her up like a rag doll and throwing her carelessly, endlessly down the mountain. Her body catapulted over and over in the raging torrent of snow, her eyes closed, her mouth silently screaming as she flailed within the fury of the avalanche.

Then suddenly Eva felt like she was floating in the clouds. She was moving, slightly swaying, as if she were gliding on her back in the sea, looking up at the dark and cloudy sky. She gulped for air whenever she felt herself surface from the great white waves. She tried to call out over the deafening roar. The whiteness turned to blackness and engulfed her.

She dreamed that she was lying in the snow, looking up at the sky . . . she was talking to Tobias . . . she was trying to explain to him about the camp fire, her urgent quest, but her words were unclear and all in the wrong order. Her panic rose and then her dream pulled her back into darkness. *I'm so tired . . . it must be time to rest . . .*

Lora tapped at Eva's cheeks, "Eva."

"Hey . . ." Eva said, slowly.

Lora wasn't in my dream.

Eva was on her back once more, but this time she could see she was just inside the open front doors of the Academy. It was dark outside but she could make out the snowmobile pulled up almost inside the doors. "Eva, can you hear me?"

"Yes," Eva said, struggling to sit up as Lora held her gently. The Professor was there too, and the nurse she'd met on her first day at the Academy.

"Eva, what do you remember?" the Professor asked her.

"Remember?" Eva asked, in a daze. She looked out at the snowmobile again, and then down at her snow suit, still smothered in wet snow.

What happened? Where's the cave and the camp fire?

The avalanche!

Eva slowly started to recall what had happened. How she'd nearly made it to the camp fire on the mountain when the avalanche struck. She was swimming in snow, searching for air. Every time she thought she was safe, it pulled her back under.

"Do you remember how you got back here?" the Professor asked her.

"I . . . did someone bring me back?" she said.

"Yes," Lora said. "You were found unconscious outside just a moment ago, someone left you and the snowmobile there."

"No . . . I didn't see anyone. I was alone the whole time," Eva said.

"There were track marks leading away, but it's snowing too heavily now to follow them," the Professor said.

Eva looked at them all, confused.

"Seems you have a guardian angel out there," the nurse said, giving Eva a drink of water. "You've been very fortunate."

"Yeah . . ." Eva said, not knowing what to make of it. She thought she recalled talking to someone, the sensation of being carried . . . *but by who? By whoever it was out there with that camp fire, that's who.*

"We had a search party out there looking for you, we had no idea where you were," Lora said. "You wouldn't want to be trapped out on the mountains at night, you'd freeze to death."

"I—I'm sorry if you were worried," Eva said. "I left a note with Gabriella."

"She fell back asleep and when she woke up the note was hidden under her bed and she'd forgotten about it," Lora explained. "We only found it later when we got worried about you being missing."

That'd be right. Thanks for nothing, Gabriella.

"And then Jedi thought to review your dream recording

so we realized what you were trying to do," Lora said.

Eva sighed deeply. "I just had to see, to get out there, to feel like I was actually *doing* something . . . I can't explain it. I dreamed I had to go."

SAM

"**H**ow do you think it ended up here?" Xavier asked, tucking the Gear into his backpack as they ran back through the tunnel toward the control room. "Being hidden in the war like that?"

"Maybe one of the scientists who worked here saw it and wanted to study it," Sam said.

"Or they wanted to steal it from some place," Xavier said. He led the way into the control room.

"Yeah, who knows . . ." Sam swallowed hard as he stood and looked out across the factory. The dust cloud still blocked the view below, and down the end from where they'd come, the glow of the German team's flashlights were looking about the aircraft frames and machines, carrying out a thorough search for them.

"They've passed under us," Sam said. That was the good news.

The bad news was there was now *another* set of flashlights. These lights were different. They were brighter, throwing out a whiter light, piercing the darkness like lasers. The other difference was that they were coming from the other end of the massive underground factory.

A second group is down here.

"What's that?" Xavier asked.

"Not what, but who," Sam said. "And I'll bet you that it's the Enterprise."

"They weren't in my dream," Xavier said, his nose to the glass.

"I didn't see them either," Sam agreed.

"What's the good of seeing the future if it's not what happens?" Xavier said, his voice starting to falter.

"As we change things from how we dreamed them, so the reality changes," Sam explained.

"Well, that's great, about my dad. I mean—he might be OK now."

"Yep."

"But now what do we do?"

Sam looked around. They had maybe two minutes before either side would be at their position. Not long enough to do much of anything. There were no other exits that he could see.

"We need a diversion," Sam said, moving over the control panels that ran along the length of the gantry. Before them were a few dozen dials.

"Think these still work?" Xavier said.

"Let's check it out," Sam said, and together, they started flicking switches.

The darkness whirred into life.

Immediately, both the Germans and Enterprise opened fire, each quickly realizing in the fog of the dust that they were not alone and becoming engaged in a firefight with each other that sent bullets sparking off aircraft fuselage pieces and immense heavy-steel pieces of old machinery. Several of the office windows cracked but did not break.

With the last switch, Sam could hear the deep cough of big diesel generators starting up—and then the ear-splitting sound as one of them exploded. Even more dust erupted around them, the sight backlit by a fire sparked from the diesel fuel. The belch of flame caused an ancient sprinkler system to creak into life and water rained down into the factory. The two sets of lights at either end of the factory now moved fast and frantically, zigzagging across the vast room as shots continued to ring out.

"That's definitely a diversion!" Sam muttered as they ducked for cover. "Keep trying stuff!" he said as they crouched underneath the control desk. Xavier pummelled the remaining switches and buttons above him.

Finally—movement.

The entire control room began to move slowly once more, the rails in the ceiling shaking with the effort.

Out on the factory floor, amongst the mayhem of the firefight playing out, other machines had groaned into life, including a conveyor belt carrying a wingless aircraft fuselage right past the office and toward the Enterprise team.

"Wow!" Xavier said, his nose pressed up to the glass, looking at the aircraft passing by. They resembled UFOs more than traditional-looking aircraft. "They're complete but for the wings."

"And that helps us because . . ." Sam asked.

"They're Horten Ho 229s—amazing," Xavier marvelled. "My dad would have loved to see these!"

By the flashing red light that cast the scene in an eerie glow, Sam wondered if his friend was going nuts in the heat of the battle raging below.

"Focus, Xav!" Sam said. "We're headed for those Enterprise guys, who're going to search in here as soon as the control room gets close enough."

"We can ride out in a cockpit!" Xavier said.

"A cockpit?"

"In one of the planes!"

"We don't know where that conveyor is going," Sam said.

"It's gotta be better than where this control room is going," Xavier said, pointing to flashes of machine-gun fire.

"OK, good point," Sam said. "How do we do this?"

34

ALEX

After expertly weaselling his way to the front of the line at the gate, Alex despaired at the size of the Berlin Zoo. *How will I ever find them in here? What if I've already missed Stella's secret meeting?*

He'd almost not believed his luck when he'd spied some Agents in the crowd near the monkey enclosure. Sticking to them like glue, Alex had watched in awe as Stella and her team had converged next to an ordinary-looking garden bed and then blasted through it, not even caring who was watching. Without turning a hair, they'd casually roped down through the hole in the garden. As Alex came up close for a look, he saw there had been a concrete slab structure underneath a metre or so of topsoil.

Smiling to the curious tourists who were beginning to look over, he crept to the hole and looked in. He couldn't see anything but darkness, and he held onto a rope to peer down into—*a factory?* By the dull flashlight illumination somewhere deep below, he could make out a conveyor belt, stacked high with what looked like plane parts that ran the length of the factory floor.

What has Sam gotten himself into now?

It took only a moment for Alex to make his decision. He pulled out the descenders he'd stowed in his backpack, clipped them onto the nearest rope and flipped over the edge into the darkness below.

He began cranking the descenders, hand over hand but plummeted to the floor as he lost control of one and fell fast—saving himself the bump to earth with a final pull on the rope. *Man, that was close!*

Alex found himself in the midst of large crates, the floor covered in the dirt and discarded trash from years before. He threw himself behind a mound of boxes to take a moment to orient himself.

Right, time to find out what's really going on.

He pulled out a flashlight but stopped dead in his tracks as he heard a voice. Not just any voice, but the voice of someone, something that dripped with malice and such anger that Alex involuntarily shrank from the sound of it.

Forcing himself to inch forward, Alex took his courage in both hands and slowly peered around the corner of the boxes. There, in the darkness was an even darker shadow in the shape of a masked man. From everything he'd ever heard about him, he had no doubt. This was Solaris.

Why did I come down here? Stupid, stupid! I'm going to get myself killed.

His fear swam before his eyes as he tried to listen to the

voice as it spoke into a radio receiver.

"You know the penalty for failure," Solaris spat out. "Find the boy, find the Gear. Take all necessary measures. I expect success from you, Stella."

Alex gasped and his hands flew to his mouth to hold in the noise.

Stella? I knew it! She's a dirty, double-crossing . . .

Solaris swung around in the darkness, pacing back and forth. Alex held his breath and willed his pounding heart to be quiet. After a moment that stretched forever, Solaris turned away and just like that, he was gone into the shadows.

Alex sank to his knees, relief and panic flooding through him in equal measure.

Stella . . . working for Solaris. That's who she met with in my dream. I have to tell Jack and Mom.

Alex ran back to the ropes, grabbing the high-powered hydraulic ascenders he'd also liberated from the Enterprise stores. He snapped them onto the line and pushed the button, instantly pulled up toward the light above. He was nearly there when clicking noises rang out around him and lights flickered on throughout the factory. A loud grinding directly below him made him look down. The conveyor belt was now moving!

He flung himself up over the lip of the hole. As he was still trying to make sense of everything that was happening, he heard the unmistakable crack-patter of gunfire, along with long muzzle flashes of weapons.

Alex pulled himself back and moved away from the hole, whipping out his phone. There were three missed calls from Phoebe.

He pressed her number, impatient for the call to be answered. "Come on, come on . . . pick up . . ."

"Alex?"

"Mom, listen, I'm—"

"Stella and her Agents are at the zoo," Phoebe began.

"I'm at the Berlin Zoo," Alex said at the same time.

"And they—"

"I know, Mom, listen, *please*. Sam must be here too, down in an underground factory or something. And they've started shooting!"

"What?" Phoebe said.

"Stella and her thugs are down in this big basement thing, shooting!" Alex's voice rose to a shout.

"Alex, Agents don't shoot—" Phoebe said.

"Listen!" Alex held his phone over the hole in the ground so that his mother would get the full effect of the firefight playing out below. "Now, does that not sound like a war zone to you?!"

"I don't understand . . ." Phoebe said, her voice trailing off.

"And there's more, I saw Solaris!" Alex replied.

"What? Alex, please, I want you to stay out of danger!"

"Solaris is down there!" Alex yelled. "And Stella's

working for him!"

"What did you say?" Phoebe said quietly. "It sounded like you said—"

"I did."

SAM

Xavier seemed to be having the time of his life in the middle of this gunfight, while Sam kept his lips shut tight and grabbed onto the plane with white knuckles.

No sooner had they jumped from the steel staircase landing of the control room, they were crammed inside the cockpit of a half-finished aircraft, Xavier seated in front of Sam. Xavier tried furiously to find the lever to slide the canopy into its closed position, only to discover it was not working.

"I think it only closes with the power of the engines," Xavier said, tugging at the canopy. "Or it's stuck from age."

"Keep your head down!" Sam whispered to Xavier as the aircraft approached the Enterprise Agents, the cockpit passing their enemies at head height.

Sam peered over the edge of the grimy front section of the canopy and could see he was right—they were Agents, at least ten or more, and Stella was yet again leading them. She was in a covered position behind a stack of aircraft landing gear, while an Agent lay next to her, wounded. She gestured to small groups of Agents at either side who silently fanned out, while she remained with the middle group.

"What do we do?" Sam asked, thankful for the deafening noise of the rusty machinery. Ahead, the conveyor shuddered on, although it couldn't last indefinitely. There was something else though . . . *a glow?*

"What's that?" Xavier asked.

"Daylight?" Sam said.

About fifty metres ahead there was a large, ragged round hole blasted through the ceiling, through which several zip lines hung down.

"Must be where the Enterprise came in," Sam said. Behind them, the gunfire died down a little as the opposing forces reassessed their strategy.

"Are we still inside the zoo grounds?" Sam whispered.

"We'd have to be—it's massive," Xavier said.

"Then how about we try climbing their ropes to get out of here?" Sam suggested.

"They'll pick us off," Xavier said. "And anyway, you ever tried to climb a rope without the right equipment?"

Sam had, and it was virtually impossible.

"We need a way out," Sam said. They were nearly at the blown-out hole above.

The gunfire behind them abruptly ended. Either Hans and his men had been killed or they'd run.

"Ha!" Xavier said, fumbling about on the controls in front of him.

"Ha?" Sam turned from Xavier to the front as he thought he heard a crashing sound ahead. "Oh, man—the conveyor ends soon!"

"Do you trust me?" Xavier said.

"Xav, we're going to tip off the end of the conveyor up ahead, so I think we're going to have to make a grab for those ropes."

"Sam, do you trust me?" Xavier repeated.

"Yeah . . ."

"Then buckle up," Xavier said coolly.

"What? You want to strap in for the crashlanding ahead?" Sam's head was spinning, trying to work out what to do. They'd jump out of the plane and straight into the waiting arms of the Enterprise.

"No," Xavier said, clipping on his four-point harness as Sam did the same. "But I don't want to be thrown from the seat as we pass through that hole."

"Thrown from the seat as we—what?" Sam stammered.

Out the corner of his eye, a shadow moved toward them. The mask came into view and Sam knew they had not outrun Xavier's nightmare. Solaris raised his arm and pointed at Xavier.

Before Sam could yell out, Xavier reached over to grab two yellow handles—and pulled on each simultaneously. What happened next was a blur.

Sam hung on and screamed. Fire raced toward them as they shot into the air, missing the ragged edge of the blast hole in the ceiling by mere millimetres, and then rocketed through into the daylight above.

"Arrrgghh!" Sam shouted.

"Yeeeee-haaaaaaaa!" Xavier cried.

They flew upward and high into the sky, for what seemed like hundreds of metres—then there was a *BANG!* behind them and a parachute was deployed.

"Holy cr—"

"Arrrgghh!" Xavier screamed, a belated reaction to their precarious situation.

Below them, the immense grounds of Berlin Zoo spread out like a tourist map, people milling about like tiny ants. With the massive silk parachute above them, the ejection seat swayed gently with the breeze, the smell of the rocket propellant filling the air as they fell gently toward the ground below.

"So that's what it feels like to be shot out of a cannon," Sam said, holding onto the edges of the seat harness.

"I wish I'd filmed that . . ." Xavier murmured, laughing nervously.

"Ah, Xav, any way to steer this thing?" Sam asked, looking over the edge as they dropped toward an enclosure with a couple of large trees in the middle and a high wall all around. *I didn't think I had a problem with heights but . . .*

"Steer?" Xavier asked.

"We're headed for an enclosure," Sam said, hearing now the screams and yells of people below as they finally became aware of the drama that had been unfolding beneath their feet.

A flash of orange and black slinking through the foliage below kicked their collective déjà vu into full flight.

"It's the tiger enclosure!" Xavier shouted. "Quick, lean to the right!"

They both did so, but it was no use. The harness had them strapped in tight.

CLICK.

Xavier hit the clip and the harness unbuckled, and they shifted way to the right of the seat to the point of—

"Argh!" Xavier slipped off and Sam lunged, grabbing his friend's wrist with one hand and the harness shoulder strap with the other. Screams from onlookers rippled out like a wave below them.

Xavier was dangling, hanging on only by an arm-in-arm wrist lock with Sam.

The shift of their weight caused the ejection seat to tip and tilt wildly, their trajectory veering away from the enclosure.

"Xavier, watch out!" Sam called out. "We're gonna land!"

They overshot the tiger enclosure, the paved ground below looming up fast as—

RIP!

Sam looked up, horrified to see that the silk canopy above had torn with the sudden change of weight pulling on one side of the para cords.

They were dropping too fast.

Xavier looked up at Sam, wide-eyed, and in unison their arms slid apart as they struggled to keep hold of each other.

Sam saw Xavier land some ten metres below, feet first into a huge lagoon in another enclosure. He swiftly broke the surface of the green water and swam for shore—then toward a ladder set into the lagoon's outer wall as a hippopotamus started charging for him.

"SAM!"

Sam heard his name but couldn't see who was calling him, then his eyes locked onto the black figure of Solaris.

Solaris stood below, waiting with an air of inevitability. An insistent alarm rang out across the zoo as bystanders scattered, running from the scene as Solaris threw fire in every direction.

Are those Enterprise Agents with him?

Sam twisted in his seat, trying to work out what he was seeing.

WHOOSH!

One blast of Solaris' fire weapon and the parachute was in tatters, sending Sam tumbling toward the ground.

And then the fire came again and again, flames shooting so close Sam could feel the searing heat scorching his body. Parts of the chair were on fire. The heat was intense.

"Get away from me!" Sam shouted but his voice was whipped away by the pounding wind. He plummeted through the air, strapped into the ejection seat that was twisting and turning and burning as it fell.

No, not this way.

Please.

Despair washed over Sam as he fell. He curled his body inward, making himself small, blocking out the flames and the rushing wind, and *him*.

He crashed to earth in a crunch of steel and leather, and rolled painfully across the ground. He struggled to move, and felt a shadow fall across his face. All he could hear was Solaris' rasping breath. He saw the masked face come closer . . .

This is it. My nightmares have finally come true.